I0783653

The Marked & The Menaced

A Vexia Novella

Mallory Wanless

ISBN:

Paperback:
979-8-9888284-7-1

Ebook:
979-8-9888284-8-8

content warning

To those who think they'll never find love.
Don't lose hope.
It could be waiting for you right around the next corner.

Mom, if you're reading this, please stop here.
You won't like this one. It's spicy...

1

OLIVER STARED OUT THE window beyond the bar, absentmindedly stirring the cauldron of stew over the firepit, dreading the night's itinerary. The Thieves' Guild would be coming to collect their monthly payment, as they did every Black Moon and he was ill-prepared.

Well, he was quite prepared. He simply didn't want to do what he knew they'd expect of him.

Oliver was the firstborn son of Chantrelle and Enoki, two of the most notorious grifters in the realm. They were so skilled in their grifts that their marks rarely knew they'd been robbed until days—sometimes even weeks—later. Oliver had inherited that gift from his dutiful parents, who quickly roped him into their jobs as soon as he could walk and coherently talk. He was a master grifter by the time he'd gotten his first chest hair. He'd nearly surpassed his parents' skill when his brother had started showing symptoms of the sickness.

At first, it had just been a small cough. Dry, but unwilling to let up. It slowly evolved into something wet and took hold of Matheu's lungs, causing him to have a whooping cough that never truly receded. The day Matty had begun to cough blood was the day their parents had sought the Guild's assistance. That was the day they'd become eternally indebted to the Thieves' Guild.

While under the leadership of a man called Tameer, the Guild had thrived and all its members had prospered. But as Tameer moved to make drastic changes—like banning child labor, gods forbid—many of the older members who relied on the labor of others pushed back, ultimately staging a coup and driving Tameer away. Rumor had it, he'd been killed, although Oliver wasn't convinced. Tameer had been a very resourceful man, according to the stories. It seemed unlikely that he would have been so easily disposed of. However, Oliver had never actually met the man. The moment his brother's illness had taken a turn, Oli had dropped everything to tend to his every need. Their parents began working jobs for the Guild in exchange for medicine that kept Matty's symptoms in check. They had no cure, but they offered him relief and comfort. If that was all they could find for Matty, then Oliver knew their parents would do whatever it took to make sure he got the medicine every month.

It had been a decent enough system—if a bit exhausting—until their parents were tasked with a near-impossible job that landed them in a merchant's dungeon. Oliver still hadn't learned the extent of the assignment. Their parents had steadfastly refused to give him any details about the job, and when they'd been unable to complete the assignment, the Guild had left them in that damned dungeon to suffer the consequences of their failure. On top of that, without completing the job, the Guild was under no obligation to fulfill their end of the bargain: i.e. provide Matty's medicine.

Three months ago, when their parents had been captured, Oliver had reacted... poorly. He'd stormed into the Guild's tavern, demanding a face-to-face with the leader and a plan for how they intended to free his parents. For his trouble, he had been soundly beaten and left in a bloody heap in the gutter behind the bar. He'd spent three days nursing his wounds—and bruised ego—at a brothel, ignoring the women, preferring the solitude of a room and the comfort of a bottle each night. Matty had found him on the floor beside the bed, empty bottle clutched in his fist, stewing in his rage at the knowledge of what he was going to have to do.

Oliver was a gifted grifter, but he *hated* it. He loathed tricking people into trusting him. He despised stealing from them. His only blessing was knowing the jobs his parents took were against marks that truly deserved their wrath. Oliver wasn't a good person, not by any stretch of the imagination, but he refused to be a terrible one. The Thieves' Guild didn't give a shit. They'd send him after whoever they wanted, for whatever they wanted, regardless of his personal qualms.

Matty force-fed him broth and bread, sobering him up, and accompanied him to the Guild the next night. The assignment they'd been given was unpleasant, but not the worst thing

Oliver had ever done. They conned a noble out of his mother's fortune the next week, bringing the bounty to the Guild in exchange for Matty's medicine.

The next few months had been a series of the same. Grift some asshole out of their fortune, trick some fool into signing away their life savings, then convince a little old lady that her collection of gems would be safer in their "storage facility" than in her own home. He'd drank himself into a stupor for a week after that one.

"Ye got visitors." Geoffree smacked the open window between the kitchen and the bar, shaking Oliver out of his reverie.

"Fuck," Oliver muttered. Stirring the stew one last time, he nodded to Geoffree. "Coming, boss."

Tameer had spent the majority of the last few months in Ravendale with Irena and Dimitri. Well, truthfully, he'd spent the time playing with the baby. While Tameer had no desire to have children of his own, being an uncle was by far the most fun he'd had in a *very* long time. Possibly ever. That little boy was the most animated, adorable creature and he was so clever! At only six months old, he had the entire castle staff wrapped around his chubby little finger.

Tam loved watching the little prince squeal with delight when his mother entered the room. Or fling his toys just to watch his father dive to retrieve them from the floor. Nicolette, Irena's handmaiden, was an excellent partner in crime, helping Tam to sneak the little prince out while his parents were on dates or at boring meetings. The King and Queen of Mistfall had busy days filled with endless meetings, but the little prince needed to play and explore. Tameer was more than willing to take him on all the adventures. They visited the various gardens, played in the river, and strolled through the observatory where Dimitri had proposed to Irena. It was a lovely way to spend his time, but Tameer knew it couldn't last forever. As much as he was enjoying his time in the capital, this wasn't his real life.

He ambled into the library one evening to find Irena cuddling her son in one of the overstuffed loveseats by the fireplace, gazing down in awe at her beloved miracle.

"Good evening, Your Majesty," he said with a dramatic bow.

"Hush, you." She swatted at him with her free hand, not looking up from her precious babe's face. "I know why you're here and I don't accept."

"I wasn't aware that I needed royal approval to go home," Tameer teased, but he took her hand, sitting on the low table before her, squeezing her fingers gently until she looked him in the eye.

A bright gloss shimmered in her eyes, tears lining her lashes as she tried to hide her true feelings. "I'm not ready for you to leave." Her voice cracked on the final word.

Tameer moved to sit beside her on the loveseat, pulling her and her child into a warm embrace. "I know, love, but I can't stay here forever. As much as I've enjoyed being here with you and your little family, I need to get home. You know the kind of trouble Leah gets up to when I'm not around to temper her. Not to mention, that giant of a guard she's fucking... they've probably busted holes in the walls by now. I need to go make sure my room in still in tact. And probably start looking for my own place." His thoughts trailed off. Tameer was a very confident man. Some might say *too* confident. But of late, as his adopted sisters have found love and paired off, he'd started to feel like a third—or rather fifth—wheel. He was thrilled for them both, truly, but selfishly, Tameer worried where that left him.

Irena sighed, leaning back and resting her head in the crook of Tameer's shoulder. "You could just stay. We have plenty of room here. Hells, you could have an entire tower to yourself, if you wanted. We could give you a title and position in court. Make you the leader of whatever branch of whatever you want." She shifted, as though trying to melt into him. "Just stay."

Tameer pressed a soft kiss into the crown of her blonde hair. "I appreciate the offer, little sister, but I need to make my own path. And you need time with your future husband. Plan that damn wedding, already. Preferably before this little one can walk you down the aisle." Tameer reached over her shoulder and gently stroked the little prince's cheek. "That's my job, anyway."

"You're damn right. So plan to be back here in the spring."

"Yes, Your Majesty."

2

"WHAT'S THE JOB?" OLIVER sat down, straight-backed in the chair, glaring at the Guild emissaries lounging across from him.

"What kinda greeting is that? And for your favorite coworkers no less." The woman was a head shorter than Oliver, although the enormity of her violent purple afro made her seem much taller.

Her twin brother offered a feigned look of disappointment at Oliver's lack of welcome. "I would've thought you'd be happy to see us. Since we come with instructions and the key to your brother's treatment. But if you aren't interested..." His voice trailed off as he took a pointed drag from his tankard, eyeing the door as though he was more than willing to leave without conveying the Guild's message. Leaving Oliver without a job and therefore without a way to earn his brother's medicine.

"What do you want from me?" He sighed in defeat, resting his head in his hands. "We aren't friends. Hells, we're barely coworkers." Sitting back, his gaze hardened, locking eyes with them both in turn before continuing. "You deliver assignments and then return to the Guild with the bounty once I've finished the job. You're glorified messenger ravens."

Eva looked ready to lash out, enraged by the insult, but Evan's answering cackle was what broke the tension at their table.

"Ravens," he chuckled, wiping his eyes with the back of his hand. "That's a good one." Without another word, he pulled a rolled parchment from his pocket and slide it across the table to Oliver. "The job needs to be done by the week's end. The target is said to be on the move and arriving in town from the capital today or tomorrow."

Oliver subtly glanced around the room, ensuring no one was paying attention to him, then slid his finger under the wax seal, breaking it and quickly surveying the instructions written—in code, of course—within.

"This is a kill mission," he whispered, his tone a mixture of confusion and disgust. "I don't kill."

"You will if you want your brother's medicine," Eva smirked, tipping her tankard in some sort of twisted salute.

"Wait until you see who the mark is." Evan leaned forward in his seat, genuinely giddy at the prospect.

Gods, how could this job possibly get any worse?

Oliver unrolled the rest of the missive.

What the fuck? "Tameer?"

Tameer rarely found himself lacking in confidence, but as he dragged his feet on the unpaved road back to Vexia, he couldn't help feeling pretty damn pitiable. He'd stayed with Irena far longer than he'd intended, under the guise of being the good uncle. In truth, he'd been dreading coming back. Now that Ash was living with him and Leah, Tameer often felt like an unwelcome guest in his own home. It was unfair, and he knew if he simply mentioned it to Leah, she would work to find a better balance for them all, but it was her place too. Hells, it was her home *first*. She'd practically forced Tameer to live there with her all those years ago when he'd been unceremoniously kicked out of the Guild. They'd sent assassins after him over and over for a while, but when the assassins kept coming up dead, and Tameer kept breathing, the Guild finally quit trying.

Tameer had never intended on living with Leah forever. Maybe this was the gods' way of telling him it was time to strike out on his own. He'd always been quick on his feet—and even quicker with his tongue. He could start fresh in a new city. Build his own life. The gods might even see fit to bless him one last time and see him at the top of a new guild, running the thieves of a new city. He did enjoy being in a leadership position.

Minus all the backstabbing and political games that came along with it.

Vexia came into few as Tameer turned the final corner on the path through the woods. From the outside, the town looked almost quaint. Small homes built of moss covered stone with wood-framed windows and front doors that were nearly always left open or at least ajar. Cobblestone steps from the doors to the gravel road that served as the main thorough faire as well as the market street. The majority of the residents of Vexia were criminals in some capacity: retired, recuperating, or in hiding from some form of law enforcement or another.

The laws in Vexia were simple:

Don't rob from your neighbor.

Don't kill your neighbor without just cause.

Don't be a snitch.

Tameer couldn't help the grin that tugged at his tired lips at the sight of the town. He might not have intended to stay in Vexia when he'd joined Leah, but gods take him, he didn't want to leave.

I guess that kills any plans at becoming a crime lord elsewhere, he thought ruefully, embracing the smile that took up permanent residence on his face. With a bit more pep in his step—as Dimitri might have said—Tameer sauntered into town, heading straight for the only inn in town. Vexia might be home, but Tameer was certain that he didn't want to spend another night listening to his best friend cry out in ecstasy while that giant of an ex-guard railed her. Tameer shuddered at the thought.

"Well, look who finally decided to show up." The grin on the petite woman's face belied the chastisement in her words as Maddie, the innkeeper, came out from behind the counter to pull Tameer into a warm embrace. "We were starting to think you'd never come back."

Tameer returned her hug, chuckling into her braids. The woman—part pixie, if the rumor mill was to be believed—barely came up to Tameer's chest, with sparkles in her eyes and an ever-present smile on her face. Tameer got the impression that the smile was hiding something, but he'd learned that it was easier to wait and let people spill their secrets than to force them out before they were ready. "I could never stay away too long. I was actually hoping you might have a room for me?" He gave her what he hoped was a pleading look, one that conveyed desperation without needing further explanation. The whole town knew about Leah and Ash. Those two were about as shy as wild animals in heat.

Maddie gave Tameer a knowing smile and nodding, releasing him and circling back behind her desk to check the guest book. "Looks like I've got a few rooms available." Taking a key off the wall, she turned with a wink and said, "I'll put you in the Snowdrop room." The key ring she handed him held a heavy iron key attached to a wooden carving of a snowdrop flower. The flower itself seemed simple enough, but Tameer couldn't help thinking that Maddie was trying to imply something with this specific flower.

When she didn't say anything else, however, Tameer shrugged internally and thanked her. "How much do I owe you?"

"Not a damn thing," she insisted. "I will not take your coin. However, if you want to pay in trade, I could use some help deciphering Gran's books. She left this place in a bit of mess."

"Left?" Tameer froze mid-step. Gran was an institution in Vexia. One of the founding townsfolk. Why the hells would she leave?

"Oh, shit. I'm so sorry, Tam. I forgot you weren't here. She passed, love. Two months back. The pox finally took her." Maddie glanced down at her hands, fidgeting with her nails. Tameer followed her gaze to see the woman's cuticles had been torn to shreds. She'd clearly been stressed and taking it out on them for weeks.

Tameer stepped behind the counter and pulled Maddie into another, firmer hug. "I'm so sorry, Maddie. I had no idea. I would've been here sooner. Your gran was an amazing woman. I don't know how this town will get on without her." Rubbing his hand slowly up and down the length of her spine, Tameer felt the tension Maddie had clearly been carrying for a while.

Tameer didn't know much about Maddie's people. Gran had been in Vexia since the beginning, running the Inn and helping make the town what it was. She had children, obviously, but Tameer had never seen any of them. Maddie was the only one of Gran's kin he'd ever met.

When he pulled back, Tameer saw the glistening of tears in Maddie's eyes. "I will be more than happy to help you untangle

Gran's books. And anything else you need. I'm at your disposal."

Maddie swiped a hand under her eyes. "Thanks. I keep thinking I'm all right, then something happens and it hits me all over again."

"That's grief, babe. It never really goes away. It does get easier, though. It just takes time, unfortunately." Tameer offered her a soft smile. "Do you want me to take a look at those books now?"

Maddie returned his smile then scrunched her nose. "Thanks, but no. You stink. Did you walk the whole way here? You need a bath. And you definitely need to see Leah and get some clean clothes. You can't live in those gross, sweaty things forever," Maddie teased. The tears faded from her eyes as she poked fun at him. "Besides, it's the middle of the afternoon, they can't possibly be having sex right now, can they? They have to take breaks for food and rest at some point, right?"

"You'd be surprised," Tameer groaned.

3

O LIVER GROANED, ROLLING OVER in his too-small cot, glaring at the sun that had the nerve to shine cheerfully through their small window. Matty perked up at the sound, pushing up from the chair he'd been lounging in and setting his book aside to give Oliver his full attention.

"What happened? You were completely obliterated when you lumbered in last night. By the smell of it, you drank your weight in ale. I take it the Guild sent the next job?" Matty knew the arrangement, much to Oliver's chagrin. He'd desperately tried to keep that information from him, thinking it was safer to protect his brother and allow at least one of them some semblance of normalcy. Unfortunately, that was basically impossible with their parents locked away. Oliver had failed to concoct a reasonable explanation for why their parents would be gone and unreachable for an indeterminate amount of time. The truth had won out.

Oliver desperately wished he could roll over and forget everything. Go back to fantasy dream land where a gorgeous man had been rubbing lotion over his tight muscles and massaging away all his stress and worries. Life, however, was never that kind, and Vexia was far too loud for sleeping in. Below their foxglove-framed window, the market was alive with energy and irritatingly vocal merchants shouting out their daily sales.

"Talk to me." Matty shoved a steaming cup of coffee under Oliver's nose. "What's the job?"

Sitting upright and accepting the coffee with another groan, Oliver exhaled slowly as he debated how to respond. He'd spent the first half of the night trying to find a way out of the assignment and the second half drinking himself into a stupor so he wouldn't have to think about what he was being forced to do. Oliver had never killed someone. *Never.* He didn't think he even had it in him to inflict that kind of violence on another living creature. But it was Tameer or his brother, so it would have to be Tameer.

Sighing one last time, Oliver locked eyes with his brother. "It's bad, Matty." No point in lying or sugar-coating things. They were in this shit together and it would likely take both of them to do this job. "The Guild has tasked us with—" He dropped his voice even though they were alone in their private room at the end of the hall in the small inn. "—killing Tameer."

Matty blinked for a few moments, mouth hung open, then to Oliver's surprise, he started laughing. Not just laughing, the man started cackling as tears rolled down his eyes; pure, unadulterated joy in his voice. Oliver gaped at his brother while the man took an absurd amount of time to calm down and regain control of himself.

"By the gods, Oli. I thought you were serious for a minute there. That was a good one." He chuckled once more, wiping his eyes and shaking his head. "Truly though, what's the job?"

Oliver's gaze didn't falter. "That *is* the job. The twins came by the tavern last night. Check the missive yourself if you don't believe me." He fished the tattered parchment from his pocket and tossed it onto the small wooden table before his brother. Stretching, Oliver drew several pops from his spine that normally would have been cathartic but in this moment, nothing could have helped him feel relaxed or remotely calm.

Matty's eyebrows shot up as he took the scrap of parchment and scanned the coded message. "Fuck. They're serious. How do they even know he's still alive? No one's seen him in what, a year?"

"Apparently, he was spotted in Ravendale last month with Queen Irena. The Guild is worried that he's becoming too influential and they want to cut him out for good."

"Why us? We aren't killers."

Oliver had asked that very same question last night. "According to the ever delightful Eva, the Guild thinks we will be the most highly motivated. They have promised to not only secure your medicine for a year, but also aid in freeing our parents if we do this job."

"And if we fail, then we're one less thing they have to put resources into," Matty finished.

The Guild often liked to remind them that Matty's medicine wasn't cheap. It cost the Guild great pains and resources to procure it for him every month, so naturally, the family must pay in kind in order to receive the life-saving treatment.

Nodding, Oliver took a long pull on his coffee. No words were needed; they both knew the score.

"Did they at least give any advice or tips on where to find him or even what he looks like? He was gone by the time we started working for the Guild, wasn't he? I've never even seen the man." Matty glared at the crumpled missive in his hand as though it were the source of all their problems.

Oliver, who was several years older than Matheu, had been an active member of the Guild for a few years when Tameer had been climbing the ranks, primarily within Ravendale's city walls. By the time Tameer had taken full control, however, Oliver had chosen to quit the family business. It wasn't that he disapproved of his parents' lifestyle, per se, but he wanted more for himself. He wanted a choice in his life.

Naturally, his mother had been disappointed, but she'd chosen to keep *most* of her opinions to herself. His father, however, had been far more outspoken. It had driven a wedge between them for several years. Matty's illness was the thing that had brought them all back together. A common enemy, as it were.

"I've got a rough description, and they said he should be arriving in town today from the capital." Oliver looked out the window. "Fuck, it's well passed midday. He may already be here. Why did you let me sleep so late?"

Matty raised an incredulous eyebrow that said, *Like I had a choice?* but no words left his mouth.

"Right. Sorry," Oliver quickly said. "Too much ale. I'll head to the tavern and see if Geoffree knows him. That man knows fucking everyone. If anyone can point us in the right direction, it'll be him."

The tavern forever smelled of piss and ale. Oliver was certain that Geoffree poured extra ale on the floors in the early morning hours, just to ensure the stench hung around. Still nursing a bitch of a hangover, Oliver was nauseated just walking up to the door.

"If you're going to be sick, do it in the alley," he heard Geoffree call from beyond the chipped tavern door.

Matty had the balls to chuckle at his brother's misfortune, holding the door wide open to give him a full whiff of the oppressive odor that awaited them. Oliver groaned. Steeling himself against the onslaught of stomach-churning scents, he set his shoulders and crossed the threshold into his own personal hells.

"So glad ye could make it," Geoffree teased, giving them a toothy grin from his position behind the slick bar. It was not quite evening yet, but the tavern was still crowded with regulars. A few games of cards and dice took over tables around the room, while the booths along the walls were hidden in shadows and more discreet conversations. Likely deals or plans being made, agreements being brokered, money changing hands. Vexia was known for its shady citizenry, after all. If you were looking to hire for a job, this was the town to come to and Geoffree's was the tavern to start with.

Stepping up to the bar, desperately trying to ignore the way his boots slide on the-gods-only-knew-what on the sawdust strewn floor, Oliver took a seat, nodding to Geoffree as Matty remained standing behind him. They'd been living in Vexia for a couple of months now, long enough to know that people in town didn't commit unwarranted crimes against one another—generally—but that didn't mean they were going to let their guards down.

"What'll it be, lads?" Geoffree asked over his shoulder. He pulled a draft for another patron—a dwarf by the looks of that beard—then turned expectantly to Oliver. "I didn't expect to see you in here. On your day off and especially after last night." Geoffree's grin was filled with paternal mockery. He'd been the one serving Oliver after the twins had departed. Geoffree might not know what Oliver was trying to drown, but he had not problem providing the liquid. "Hair o' the dog, mayhaps?" Geoffree teased, slapping the bar at his own joke as Oliver grimaced.

"No, I'm good. We're looking for someone, actually. I was hoping you'd know him. Tameer? I heard he just got into town." Oliver tried to keep his tone as casual as possible, hoping Geoffree wouldn't read anything into it.

"Oh, aye. That's him there." Geoffree nodded his head toward a table in the back corner.

Oliver turned slowly, not to draw attention to himself as he got a good look at their target. The man was huge. A fucking mountain. His arms alone were as thick as Oliver's neck. How the hells were they supposed to kill that beast? Beside the man sat a petite woman with curly, rose gold hair. "Beside" was a bit of an overstatement. She was practically in his lap. Her hand toying with the hair at the base of his skull, twining it between her fingers. It was clear she was infatuated. Oliver instantly felt a pang of guilt at the mere thought of taking this man from the woman who clearly cared for him. Across the table from them sat another man. Partially hidden from view, thanks to the behemoth with his back to them, the other man seemed a bit uncomfortable. Almost anxious, tearing his bread to small pieces and fidgeting with his drink.

"Fuck. Do you know who that is?" Matty's whispered voice held a note of awe.

"Yeah, that's Tameer. A mountain of a man that we're somehow supposed to kill," Oliver grumbled.

"No, that woman." Matheu carefully reached behind Oliver and took one of the tankards of ale Geoffree had left for them both. Keeping an air of casualness that Oliver was struggling to feign, Matty took a swig before muttering into his tankard so only Oliver could hear. "That's Leah. The most famous and skilled assassin and poisoner in the entire fucking realm."

Fuck. Fuck. Fuck. Could this job get any worse?

Tameer had hoped that going to the tavern would mean less physical affection. Less touchy-feely nonsense. He'd really hoped for a little one-on-one time with his best friend. Instead, he was the awkward third wheel—again—while Leah practically felt up Ash in the middle of the tavern over drinks while chatting with him like it was the most natural thing in the fucking world.

Gods, he hated feeling so lonely. He hated all of this petty bullshit that kept swirling around in his head. He should be *happy* for his sisters. So why was he so bitter and unhappy for himself all the time?

And why were those guys at the bar staring daggers at the back of Ash's head?

"Leah," Tameer interrupted whatever bullshit story she was telling about whatever dumb but supposedly cute thing Ash had done recently in the kitchen while she was trying to teach him to bake. "There are two guys staring at your lover at the bar and they don't seem to happy to see him."

Ash immediately turned to look over his shoulder, but Leah caught his face and planted a deep—and rather pornographic—kiss on his lips. He looked quite dumbfounded when she pulled away, moving her lips to his ear where she likely whispered something along the lines of, "Don't look, idiot. We need to be stealthy."

Tameer leaned casually back in his chair, resting an ankle on his knee and pretending to take a long sip of his own drink while eyeing the men through his lashes. If he had to guess, they were related. Brothers most likely. The older one was cute, but grouchy. The other one almost reminded Tam of a dog. A labrador or golden retriever. Some big, happy, dopey thing that would do whatever you asked just to see you smile and maybe get a pet or a treat. It drew an unwelcomed smile to Tameer's face.

"What do you think, Tam? What's the play?" Leah's hawk eyes were fixed on him and Tameer couldn't help but feel nostalgic for a moment. They'd played this scene out numerous times over the years, facing off against debt collectors, assassins, and just general pissed off folks. It felt like coming home. The smile that tugged at Tameer's lips now was entirely welcomed.

"Normally, I'd vote for the miller's boys route, but since these two seem fixated on our own personal giant, I say we play the Drunken Daze."

The answering glint of amusement in Leah's eyes was all Tameer needed. He made a show of downing the last of his drink while Leah climbed into Ash's lap, whispering the plan into his ear while giving the tavern quite the tantalizing show. Ash finished his tankard of water—unbeknownst to their onlookers—in one loud gulp as Leah jumped and dramatically stumbled from his lap. She grabbed Tameer's hands and hauled him from the booth, pulling him to his feet and wrapping her arms around his neck.

"Le'sh go home, my luvliesh," she proclaimed. Keeping one arm firmly around Tameer's neck, she hooked the other under Ash's arm, making a show of pulling with all her might to drag him from the chair.

To his credit, Ash had become a much better actor over the last few months and managed to stumble a bit on their way to the door as well. Either that or Leah was successfully tripping him as they walked. Regardless, the ruse seemed to be working.

The grump and the puppy saw their opportunity and they were taking it. Tossing some coins onto the counter, the fools followed Tameer, Leah, and Ash out of the tavern.

A sly grin spread across Tameer's face once more. Gods, this was gonna be fun.

4

IT WAS TOO GOOD to be true, Oliver knew it, but he was never one to look a gift horse in the mouth. He and Matty followed the drunken trio out of the tavern and into the dank alley behind the tavern. With the slow grace of an unpracticed murderer—as that's exactly what he was—Oliver pulled his dagger from the sheath at his waist. The subtle hiss of the blade scraping the sheath echoed in the sudden silence of the alley.

"Where the hells did they go?" Matty's voice was barely a whisper as his shoulder brushed against Oliver's. They crouched, turning slowly to take in their surroundings as they made their way carefully down the alley.

"They couldn't have gotten far," Oliver mumbled. His eyes were quick to adjust to the darkness. Sudden movement to his right had him raising his dagger just in time to see a fist coming straight for his jaw. Dodging to the left, he could feel the wind rustle his hair as the offending hand just missed making contact.

Throwing a punch of his own, Oliver was rewarded with a man's grunt as his fist collided with someone's ribcage. Raising his dagger once more, Oliver hooked the blade, hoping to cause some serious damage to the man, putting him out of the fight so he could focus his energy on the assassin and Tameer, that mountain of a man they'd been sent to kill.

Despite his opponent's smaller frame, the man was wily as fuck. Doggedly weaving and landing several solid hits of his own. Panting, Oliver was struggling to maintain his focus. Where was Matty? He hadn't seen or heard anything outside of his own scuffle in several moments.

Fed up and frankly, pissed the fuck off, Oliver landed a low blow. Grabbing the wiry man by the shoulders, he kneed him in the balls. It was Oliver's least favorite move, but when it came to Matty's safety, nothing was off limits. The man instantly collapsed.

The female cried out farther down the alley. Oliver couldn't make out what she'd said, but she was definitely much farther away than he'd expected. Grasping the man firmly by the collar, Oliver forced him into a standing position, holding the dagger to his throat.

"Where is my brother?" Oliver demanding in the direction of the assassin's voice.

"Give me back mine first and I'll tell you," she countered, glaring daggers at him through the darkness.

"Bullshit." Oliver dug his blade in a bit deeper, causing the man—the assassin's brother, apparently—to inhale sharply.

"Fine." The woman raised her hands in a placating gesture. "Darling?" Tameer, the mountain, stepped out from behind a tower of crates, Matheu dangling in his grasp as the oaf had one monstrous hand wrapped around the back of his neck, his toes barely touching the ground.

"Let him go!" Oliver couldn't keep the panic from his voice.

"You first," the woman replied, casually flipping her rose gold hair over her shoulder as though captive exchanges were a regular Tuesday night for her.

Maybe they were.

Oliver didn't hesitate for a moment. They needed to finish the job, but it was pointless if Matty died in the process. Hells, Matty was the whole reason they were doing the job in the first place. Without him, Oliver might as well let this assassin turn her blade on him right now.

Dropping his dagger in the dirt, he stepped away from the man and raised his hands in defeat. "Please," he added quietly. "Please just let him go. Take me instead. This was my idea, anyway. If you need to hurt someone, hurt me."

Tameer stumbled forward, his balance thrown off at being suddenly released and his balls still throbbing from the kick that brute had landed. What the hells kind of man kicks another man in that most precious area? A monster, Tameer had no doubt.

Taking a few unsteady steps toward Leah and Ash, he turned to glare over his shoulder at the older of the brothers who'd attacked them in the alley.

"What do you want with us?" Tameer's voice was rougher than he would have liked, having a blade to one's throat will do that, but his eyes were focused as he righted himself.

"We didn't want you all. Just one. It doesn't matter. Please, just give me back my brother and you'll never see us again." The pleading in the man's tone was desperate. Tameer might have felt sorry for him, if he didn't feel a trickle of his own blood slipping under the collar of his kurta.

"Which one of us?" Ash's tone was gruff. He held the brother's neck firmly, but lowered the younger man enough that his feet were settled *almost* firmly on the filthy alleyway.

"Does it matter?" The man had the balls to ask questions in this situation? Tameer couldn't decide if he was impressed with the man's courage or baffled by his stupidity.

Ash said nothing in response, but his grip on the brother tightened as he lifted the younger man off the floor just enough to elicit a grunt as he struggle to catch his footing.

Raising his hands once more, the man rushed to placate their grumpy guard. "Please, please. You. We were hired to kill you, Tameer."

Tam froze for a moment. Time seemed to stand still. The man was clearly speaking to Ash. Did he think...?

"I'm sorry, love. Run that by me again." Leah stepped forward, placing herself between Ash, their captive, and the older brother. Tameer felt in the moment the half-fae assassin unleashed her compulsion magics on the man. "Who sent you to kill whom and why?"

Her voice was as thick as honey and left a sickeningly sweet taste in the back of Tameer's throat. Having grown up with her and watching her develop her powers, he'd quickly built up a tolerance to them. He could feel it now, when she turned on her compulsion. She couldn't use it on him anymore, thank the gods. Not since that time she had him make out with a shit-covered shoe as punishment for stealing her boyfriend. From then on, they'd had a *very* strict "no shared partners" rule.

The rest of the men in the alley, however, weren't quite as lucky. The older brother seemed to notice that something had changed, but he couldn't fight the compulsion anymore than a moth could fight the urge to fly directly into a flame.

"The Thieves' Guild hired us to kill him." He nodded to Ash in clarification. "Tameer, former leader of the Guild and current friend of the Queen."

Leah's eyes flicked first to Ash and then to Tameer. Annoyance and confusion flashing in her gaze. "And who told you that *that* man was the Tameer you seek?"

"Geoffree, the barkeep."

Oh for fuck's sake. Of course he fucking did. That asshole probably thought this would be hilarious.

"Tell me, darling, do you owe Geoffree money?" Leah asked, a coy smile trailing her lips.

The man shook his head, confusion on his face.

"Does he dislike you for some reason?"

"I'm his cook. I don't think he has any reason to dislike me." The man seemed genuinely perplexed by this line of questioning. "Please, ma'am, will you release my brother? He's sick. We only work for the Guild in exchange for his medicine."

At that, the younger man grunted. As though he were trying to tell his brother to shut up. Tameer looked over to see Ash had set the man firmly on the ground. With his arm around the man's neck, Ash was not quite cutting off his air supply, but definitely creating a struggle for him.

Leah was fully invested in their story, though. Waving Ash off, he released the man, who stumbled forward clutching his neck and coughing before rushing to his brother's side. "What are your names?" Tameer felt another pulse of her compulsion rush through the alleyway, likely to ensure both brothers were fully in her thrall.

"I'm Oliver," the older brother said. "And this is Matty."

"Matheu, please," he corrected, straightening his jerkin as he pulled himself to his full height, still at least a head shorter than Ash.

Tameer chuckled despite the situation. These fools were in an alley with an ex-captain of the king's guard—who they'd been misled to believe was *him*—and the most infamous assassin in all of Mistfall, and this boy had the nerve to hit on Leah in the middle of it all. It was all too hilarious. Sometimes, Tameer struggled to accept that this was his real life.

Leah sauntered up to Matheu as Ash grumbled something derogatory in the background. "Tell me, Matheu," her voice was so thoroughly laced with compulsion that his name was practically a spell all on its own. "What sort of medicine are you so desperately in need of that you would kill my darling Tameer for it?"

Matheu leaned toward her voice involuntarily. "I have red lung. The Guild sends us jobs in exchange for the medicine that keeps me alive."

"What the hells is red lung?" Ash spoke harshly, stepping up close behind Leah. Staking his claim without so many words. As if the marks all over her neck weren't clear enough indication of her current status as "taken."

Tameer joined them in the center of the alleyway, picking up Oliver's forgotten dagger and spinning the point on his fingertip. "It's a disease generally associated with the spice district south of Ravendale. Something about the way they cultivated the spices led to some very unsavory side effects. Mostly effected children a decade or so ago. I thought they eradicated it though." He eyed the men suspiciously. In this state, they would have to be highly skilled to lie through Leah's compulsion without her noticing. It seemed far more likely that they believed the things they were saying, but how the hells did this grown man have red lung, and why the fuck was the Guild sending them regular missions in exchange for treatment when the cure was easy enough to come by?

"How long have you been sick, darling?" Leah cooed, dragging a finger along Matheu's jaw. The boy shivered. He visibly shivered. *Fucking puppy dog*.

When it was clear Matheu was too smitten to speak, Oliver answered for him. "He's been dealing with this for about five years now. We've only recently started working for the Guild. Our parents were managing before hand, but they've gotten... tied up and weren't able to take this particular job."

"And our dear friend Geoffree told you that my beloved here"—Leah turned from Matheu and drape herself around Ash's neck—"was Tameer?"

Oliver merely nodded, his gaze seeming to sharpen slightly. Tameer got the impression that the man was fighting through Leah's compulsion. Interesting. He hadn't seen that happen very often, and never this quickly.

"I'm sorry, darling. You've obviously done something to upset our barkeep. This tall, imposing, sexy mountain is my mate, Ash. Not Tameer. The way I hear it, Tameer is long gone. Dead, even. Why would the Guild send you after a dead man?"

"He's not dead!" Matheu jumped in, eager to be useful once more. "The Guild said their spies saw him with the Queen in Ravendale just last month. Verified sighting."

Leah and Tameer shared a pointed look. Fuck. He should have been more careful. Leah had been warning him for weeks, but he'd grown confident. Complacent. Now the Guild was after him once more. Fuck everything.

They knew more than they were letting on. Oliver could feel the heavy weight of magic pushing against his mind, like being trapped underwater in a fishing net. He fought against it while trying to keep his expression as neutral as possible.

Matty was spilling too many secrets, but Oliver wasn't in a position to stop him. Try as he might, the net was prying secrets from him as well. He never would have revealed their truth to these strangers so freely.

That look. The look that had passed between the assassin and her brother at the mention of Tameer and the Queen. It meant something. They *knew* something. Maybe Geoffree had lied about that giant man being Tameer—an issue Oliver would address with the man if they survived the night—but Leah definitely knew Tameer. Despite her glib attitude, she was their best lead to find the man, kill him, and get the medicine Matty needed to keep breathing.

The assassin and her brother—who still hadn't bothered to give his name—had some sort of unspoken conversation before she spoke again. "Tell me more about your sickness, Matheu. I've never met an adult with red lung. Why are they sending you medicine regularly? Is your version of the illness different? Why haven't they just given you the cure?"

The cure? Oliver's heart nearly dropped out of his chest. There was a fucking *cure*?

5

OLIVER FELT IT THE moment the magic was removed. His mind was freed from the net that he'd been struggling under, the weight lifted from his shoulders. He nearly collapsed from the sudden freedom it provided as well as the metaphorical bomb the woman had just dropped.

All this time, there had been a cure. And the Guild had kept that little fact to themselves, providing a weak medicine instead to keep his family in their debt. To keep them coming back for more for *years*.

He was going to kill them.

"I see that lovely, warm, murderous gleam in your eyes." The assassin disentangled herself from the mountain—Ash, wasn't it?—and turned to face Oliver properly. "So long as your intent isn't on myself or my men, we'll be going now." Toying with her rose gold curls for a moment, she chewed on her lip and studied Matty. "If you're open to it, I think I can make the cure. I should have everything we need for it in my gardens at home. Normally, my concoctions are of a more... fatal persuasion, but I think I could whip up a healing potion. Just this once, if you're interested."

Matty stared at the assassin, mouth hung open like a love-struck fool. The woman was infamous for her skills with poison. How could he possibly be considering her offer?

"Thanks, but—" Oliver began. Matty, however, elbowed him solidly in the ribs, cutting off anymore words, as well as his supply of oxygen for a few moments.

"I would be honored, mistress." He bowed deeply.

What the fuck? The magic was gone. What the hells had gotten into his little brother? The ex-guard practically growled as he pushed himself between Leah and Matty. Her brother failed to hide the mirthful smirk that lit up his face.

Oliver tried to ignore the way his chest warmed at the sight of that smirk. The man was related to a murderer. A woman who killed for coin. Regularly and unscrupulously. For all Oliver knew, the man was a killer himself. Oliver should *not* be noticing the way the man's leathers hugged his thighs.

Fuck.

"If you're interested," Leah continued as she was shepherded away by her giant. "Come by the house. It's the cottage at the far end of Main. You can't miss it. It's the one that perpetually smells of cinnamon and sex."

An unwelcome image of the nameless man, half naked with a look of pure bliss on his face, popped into Oliver's mind, overriding his good sense. He pivoted on his heels, watching the three of them walk away. He didn't know what he was waiting for until the assassin's brother turned back and looked over his shoulder. The second they locked eyes, Oliver knew there was something about that man. He *needed* to know more about him.

Leah had called it a gleam, but Tameer saw that spark in Oliver's eyes as something else entirely. Something far hotter, in all versions of the word. It didn't help that the man was practically eye-fucking him as they walked away.

Gods, Tameer needed to get laid. It had been far too long when he was seriously considering banging the man who had just held a blade to his throat after kicking him in the jewels. Knife play wasn't his kink.

Was it...?

Glancing over his shoulder, Tameer locked eyes with Oliver. That heat was still there. The warmth of a banked fire just waiting for some wood to turn into a full-fledged inferno. The leather of Tameer's pants strained as his body willingly offered some wood of its own.

"You good?" Leah asked, wrapping an arm around his waist, seemingly oblivious to Tameer's internal struggle.

"Huh? Oh, yeah. Just..." He couldn't think of what to say. Tam's mind was racing with too many thoughts, in too many directions.

Thank the gods, Leah didn't need much from him to keep the conversation flowing. "Why would the Guild feed them some bullshit about medicine instead of just giving them the cure? It's easy enough to come by. I really think I have everything at home. Except the crocette mushrooms but I can buy that at the market in the morning. Mama Orenda should have plenty. That old witch always has everything."

"Maybe the Guild needed something from them," Ash supplied rather astutely.

Tameer often teased the man about being a large, gruff, dimwitted ogre, but he was the former captain of the King's Guard and an annoyingly quick-witted man. Hells, he'd nearly captured Leah a year ago. He'd had the chance, at least. Clever man that he was, though, he'd opted to work with her, instead. Best decision that oaf had ever made, as far as Tameer was concerned.

"Oh, that's a good point. We need to learn more about them. Can you find out more, Tam? Ask around. See where they're staying and who knows them. The older one said he works for Geoffree. We should swing back by there and see if he can shed some light on why he sent them after Ash instead of you." Leah smirked at the memory.

It was a cruel prank, but in hindsight, it was pretty hilarious. Who in their right mind would think Ash was the former leader of the Thieves' Guild? He didn't even *look* like a thief. He walked in a room and immediately drew every eye. He would make a terrible pickpocket. No finesse. No stealth. All brute force and muscles as big as babies.

"I'll see you in the morning," Tam said, turning toward the inn. Leah froze, grabbing hold of the back of his kurta and forcing him to stop as well.

"What are you talking about?"

Shit. He was hoping this would be quick and easy. Avoid any awkwardness or hard conversations. So much for that. "I, uh, well, I got a room with Maddie. I'm staying at the inn for now. Until I can find a more permanent place."

"What the hells are you talking about? You have a permanent place! It's *our* place. We've lived there for years. You might not remember, since you spent the last eight months in the castle, but *we* have a home, Tam." Leah looked truly hurt.

Tameer hated that he was the one to put that pained look on her face, but he couldn't go back to that house. Spend another night listening to the happy couple in the room next to his while he laid there, alone, wondering if he'd ever find that kind of happiness. He hated the desperate, lonely person he'd become while living with the two of them. Tameer was indescribably happy for them, truly, but the longer he lived with them, the more bitter he became for himself.

Roughing his hands over his face, trying to will the right words from his mind. When none would come, he looked mournfully at Ash. A look that said, "You get it, don't you? Please help me."

To his surprise and relief, Ash did seem to understand.

"We're a lot, love." He kept his voice soft, as though he were trying to diffuse a bomb with his words alone. "Our... nocturnal activities are quite..."

"I get it, we fuck a lot. So what?" Leah snapped. Taking Tameer's hands, she tried to hide the tears lining her lashes. "I don't want you to go."

Tameer's smile was small but held all the love and compassion of over two decades with this challenging, delightful, inspiring, infuriating woman. "I'm not *going* anywhere. I'm just not sleeping in your house anymore. I'm staying in Vexia. This town has its hooks in me. I couldn't stay away any longer if I tried. I missed you too much." He squeezed her hands, then pulled her into a hug, resting his chin in her pink hair. "But I can't listen to you yell out that man's name one more time. I might actually go insane. Or murder you both and burn the house down."

A watery laugh escaped her lips as tears dampened his kurta.

"Besides," he added with a kiss to the crown of her head. "That house was never supposed to be *ours* in the first place. You bought that beautiful place for yourself. To enjoy your retirement. I just horned in on that shit when I couldn't figure out how to live on my own."

Leah chuckled again. "And you think you're so independent now?"

"I guess we'll find out."

Sighing dramatically, Leah stepped back and wiped her face. "Fine. I don't like it, but I can accept it. As soon as you find a place, though, I'm coming through and putting all my runes on the doors and windows. I might not be living with you anymore, but that doesn't mean you're losing all of my protection. I will not accept no for an answer."

Tameer grinned. "I would expect nothing less."

6

T AMEER DEBATED HEADING STRAIGHT back to his room, but decided one last drink couldn't hurt. Based on the shit-eating grin plastered on Geoffree's face when Tameer crossed the tavern's threshold, he'd made the right choice.

"Well, you look pleased with yourself," Tameer prodded, taking a seat directly across from the barkeep as the man poured him a shot of whisky.

"Oh, aye. Was it as entertaining as I imagined in my head?" His eyes practically shone with amusement.

Tameer pulled his collar aside to reveal the dried blood he knew stained his skin from his brand new cut. "Not nearly as much fun as I would have liked."

Geoffree had the decency to look ashamed. "Shit, I'm sorry, Tam. I didn't realize things'd get violent. Oli's a good kid. Parents are grifters. I thought they'd try and knick your wallets and learn a thing or two about Vexia's unofficial rules. I didn't even know he knew which end of a blade to use."

"He definitely knew," Tameer muttered to his whisky before downing the shot. Geoffree quickly refilled it, an apology on his face. Tameer's anger eased.

Geoffree was a good man, for a retired hitter. He looked after the people he cared for and he would have never knowingly put them in danger. He couldn't have known that the Guild had tasked Oliver and Matheu with killing Tameer. Truthfully, Tam wasn't even sure if Geoffree knew about Tam's own history with the Guild. It wasn't exactly a story he liked to advertise.

Tameer accepted the second glass, thoughtfully turning it as his mind began to wander. "What do you know about them? Oliver and Matheu? How long have they been here? Where are they staying? Why are they in Vexia rather than a major city? Their skill set doesn't seem very conducive to small-town life."

Geoffree poured himself an ale, took a swig, and wiped the foam from his scraggly mustache with the back of his hand. "They got here about two months after you left. The whole family. Enoki, Chantrelle, Oliver, and Matheu."

Tameer sat up immediately at the mention of the brothers' parents. "Wait, I must have misheard you. Did you just say their parents are *Enoki and Chantrelle*?" Geoffree simply nodded. "Gods, no wonder the Guild tricked them into service. They're *legendary*. They've been grifting all over the continent for decades. They pride themselves on the 'fair redistribution of wealth' as they called it. Always stealing from the wealthiest, most arrogant and pompous assholes and leaving piles of unexplained wealth in the poorest communities. Never been caught. No one's ever even come *close*."

Geoffree raised an eyebrow, waiting for Tameer's obvious hero-worshipping to subside so he could get on with the story. Tameer shut his trap and motioned for the barkeep to continue. "Right, well, the family came through a few months back, looking for info on some merchant living just outside the capital. I was a bit surprised to hear it, since he didn't seem like their usual mark—I'd heard the stories about them too, you know—but they got what they needed and were set to be off the next day. Somethin' went wrong though."

Much to Tameer's annoyance, another patron sauntered up to the bar and Geoffree halted his tale to serve the elf and take their coin. Then a waitress needed a refill of tankards for a rowdy table and by the time Geoffree was back to continue his story, Tameer thought he might crawl out of his skin if he had to wait a second longer.

"Sorry 'bout all that." He gestured to the tavern as a whole. "Where was I?" he asked, scratching his bald head in contemplation.

"Things were going wrong for the grifter family," Tameer all but snapped at the barkeep.

A surprised eyebrow lifted, Geoffree silently chastised Tam's snippiness, but *finally* continued the story. "Aye, Enoki and Chantrelle left in the mornin', the boys stayed behind. Oliver was pissed about it, but I'm startin' to think that's just his natural state." Geoffree chuckled at the observation. "Matheu wasn't feelin' well, as is the way with that one, so Oliver stayed here with him. I'm not sure what went down. Oliver never said. But their folks never came back. Oliver and Matheu disappeared for a few days. When they came back, Oli was beat to hell, a few broken bones the old witch healer had to set. It wasn't pretty. They've been here ever since. A couple of wannabe badasses come by once or twice a month and meet with Oliver, slip him notes when they think I'm not lookin'. He always ends up wasted at the end of those nights, and again a few nights later. Whatever's goin' on with them, he ain't happy about it, but he can't find away out."

Tameer sat back in his chair, openly staring at the man. Partly because that was the most he'd ever heard Geoffree say at one time, and partly because the story he'd just told was devastating. Tam didn't need to know all the details to be able to fill in the blanks. Oliver's parents were gone. Locked up or dead, it didn't really matter because they weren't available to help and the Guild sure as shit wasn't going to do anything to get them back. Not when they had the sons of the two best grifters on the continent under their thumbs. Those wannabes would be the messengers sent by the Guild to give Oliver his assignment. Whatever the Guild was tasking him with, he clearly hated it. The Guild wasn't known for its altruistic actions—not since he'd been run out of leadership, anyway—so it was an easy assumption that the jobs Oliver had been tasked with were lucrative but likely things he'd find despicable.

The more he learned about Oliver, the more Tam couldn't help but feel drawn to the man. To help him, of course. Nothing more. He definitely didn't want to feel the man's thick arms around his waist again. Or the press of his solid chest warm against Tam's back. Oliver's breath on his neck, panting. Gasping.

Downing the last of his whisky, Tam nodded his thanks to Geoffree, tossed a few coins on the bar and left. He needed fresh air. Cool air. A quiet space to clear his head and get this man who'd just tried to *kill* him out of his mind.

The inn was a short walk from the tavern, but Tam's thoughts wandered just the same. Oliver's voice was in his head. The way he'd spoken, so gruff and possessive of his brother. Demanding. Was he like that with all the people he cared about? Would he be that controlling in all aspects of his life?

Tameer ran a hand over his face, hoping to wipe the images from his mind, already regretting that second whisky because he knew his thoughts were no longer his own. The blood typically reserved for plotting and scheming was already rapidly migrating south. Tam just prayed he could make it to his room before it became too obvious to the casual observer that his body had taken over his faculties.

Pushing the inn's door open, he nearly knocked over a patron who was exiting at the same time. Grabbing their shoulders to keep them from falling, Tameer felt it instantly.

Oliver glared at Tameer, that banked heat still smoldering in his eyes as Tameer's grip on his would-be murderer's shoulders tightened.

Fuck.

Oliver had tried staying in their room, he really had. He'd listened to the sounds of Matty's rattling breaths as his brother fell into a listless sleep for as long as he could stand.

The fucking Guild had a *cure* and they'd knowingly, willingly, *happily* kept Matty sick for years just to keep his family under their control. Forcing him and his parents to steal for them because the Guild couldn't manage those jobs without them. Those greedy fucking pricks had put Matty's life at risk over and over for *years* for their own selfish gains. He wanted to kill them. He wanted to beat them all to a bloody pulp like they'd had done to him, and then burn their precious hideout to the fucking ground.

When he couldn't take it anymore, Oliver slipped from their room, intend on drinking himself into oblivion. Matty wanted to see the assassin poisoner about a cure. While Oliver thought that was a stupid idea, Matty was steadfast and stubborn as hells. Oliver wasn't sure he could talk him out of it, and honestly, he wasn't sure he had a right to. It was Matty's life, and they'd been trapped on the Guild's leash for so long, he understood Matty's desire to jump at the first opportunity to be free.

Oliver had hoped the inn would have a bottle or two he could buy in the dining hall, but as late as it was, no one was there to serve him. He made his way to the door and was nearly accosted by the one person he'd started the night looking for and now was uncertain he should be alone with.

Tameer.

Glassy eyed and clearly a bit intoxicated himself, Tameer had a sudden death grip on Oliver's shoulders. The fire in Oliver shifted from rage to something far more passionate, but he tried to ignore it as he reached up to steady Tameer. Placing his hands on the man's ribs, just enough to make sure he didn't stumble and fall, Oliver backed farther into the inn, allowing the door to close behind Tameer.

"Hi." Tameer's breath smelled of whisky, sweet, with a hint of honey. It should have been unattractive, but Oliver couldn't help wondering for a split second what the man's lips might taste like.

"Are you all right?" he asked instead. Shifting his position, Oliver wrapped an arm around Tameer's waist and led him to a couch in the inn's den.

Tameer dropped one hand but kept the other firmly clasped around Oliver's shoulder. "Oh, I'm delightful. How are you this fine evening? Grift any black hearts lately?"

Well, damn. That was quick.

"Been asking about me, have you?" Oliver kept his tone light, but he was curious to hear how much Tameer had learned about him and his family. They were unique in their chosen targets—until Matty got sick, anyway—and not everyone agreed with his family's style.

"How could I not?" Tam countered. "Gorgeous man kicks my ass in an alley, presses me against him and leaves me feeling... things? I'd be a fool not to want to know more."

Oliver knew he should question Tameer while he was in such a forthcoming state about what all he'd been told about his family and their proclivities, but his mind had instantly fixated on the phrase "feeling things" and wouldn't be moved. Settling into the couch, Oliver leaned closer to Tameer, as though they were conspiring. "What sort of things?" Despite himself, his voice came out husky and needy.

Tameer's eyes brightened at the question and his tone. Oh, he knew exactly what he was doing. "The kinds of things a man shouldn't be thinking about in front of his sister." Leaning closer, Tameer's breath was a whisper against Oliver's ear as he spoke. "I was hoping to feel your touch, although considerably less brutally than before." He pulled back and his eyes flicked from Oliver's leg to his own lap and back, a smirk gracing that troublesome mouth.

"Are you expecting an apology?" Oliver countered, sitting up to lift his shirt and reveal the bruises already forming on his ribs. "Because as I recall, you gave as good as you got."

That smirk remained in place and Tameer's fingertips trailed gentle, teasing lines along Oliver's skin. "I always do," he promised. Leaning forward, his gaze locked with Oliver's, a question in his eyes. With the subtlest of nods, Oliver granted permission, raising his shirt higher as Tameer placed his warm hands on Oliver's hips, pulling him closer and pressing soft, chaste kisses on each and every bruise.

An unexpected gasp escaped Oliver's lips as Tameer's small kisses progressed to deeper, opened mouth kisses, licks, and bites.

"Fuck," he muttered, fisting Tameer's hair and encouraging his affections.

Laying back on the couch, Oliver offered more of himself to the man, needing to feel his hungry mouth on every inch of his skin. Tameer was eager to oblige, moving to the floor and kneeling between Oliver's feet. His sultry kisses continued as his fingers moved to the laces of Oliver's breeches. The leather was already stretched tight over his sensitive skin and Tameer seemed to be thoroughly enjoying teasing him as he brushed his hands over Oliver's swollen cock several times. Each time elicited a whimper or groan from Oliver until he felt certain he would explode.

"Gods, please. This is torture. Just kill me now," he muttered, though he wasn't sure if it was a prayer or a curse. Relief. Gods, he just needed relief.

Tameer's dark chuckle was the only response as that damned man continued to take his sweet time, toying with the laces, casually brushing his hand against Oliver's cock as it strained against its leather prison. Finally, by some blessed miracle, Tameer ceased his teasing and released Oliver from his confinement, taking him in hand and gently stroking.

"I feel like people don't say this enough, but the penis really is the most beautiful thing. Don't you think?" Tameer spoke reverently, his hand never slowing its movement, worshipping Oliver's body with both his words and actions. Flicking his tongue out, he tasted the tip, causing a shiver to race down Oliver's spine. "You are so reactive. It's amazing." He did it again. And again. And again. Each time smirking as Oliver twitched and shivered, biting his lower lip to keep from swearing. "What's the matter, Oli?" Again. "Is there something you want?" Again. "Something you need?" Again. "Something you'd like from me?" Again.

That was the last straw. Oliver grabbed a fistful of Tameer's hair, pulling his face up until their eyes were level. Growling, he bit out, "Either you take this cock right fucking now, or get the fuck out of here so I can handle this shit myself."

It was Tameer's turn to gasp and flush. Nodding like a good boy against Oliver's hold, he licked his lips, flicking his eyes back down. Oliver didn't release him as he guided Tameer back to his knees, savoring the feeling of power almost as much as the pleasure that smart mouth wrought on his flesh.

7

ORNING CAME FAR TOO quickly and with a blinding amount of sunlight. Tameer had never been a morning person, but his window in the Snowdrop room faced the morning sun, which meant a face full of bright light at dawn. He thought Maddie liked him. Now he wasn't so sure...

Groaning, he rolled over and into a warm wall of hard flesh.

Oh, right. *That* had happened. Memories flooded Tam's mind. Images of fingers gripping hips. Teeth biting lips. Shoulders. Inner thighs... The moans and sounds that they'd drawn from each other. His body was reacting already, begging for a repeat performance.

Stretching slowly, Tameer pressed his body flush against Oliver's naked form, his chest against the other man's back, wrapping an arm around his waist and carefully stroking him into wakefulness.

Placing gentle kissing up Oliver's neck, Tameer whispered into his ear. "Good morning."

Oliver practically purred as he pushed back into Tameer, his body awakening in Tam's grasp. Tilting his head to the side, giving Tam better access, Oliver was clearly looking for a little morning pleasure to start the day off right. Tameer tightened his grip, stroking more firmly, and was rewarded with a moan.

Reaching up behind him, Oliver threaded his fingers through Tameer's hair and pulled him in for a deep kiss. Rolling onto his back while never once breaking their kiss, Oliver reached down to take Tameer in his hand, matching Tam's pace.

In a matter of moments, they were both panting, no longer able to maintain the kiss as they pressed their foreheads together and fixated on the pleasure they were drawing from each other.

"Not until I tell you to," Oliver grunted as Tameer picked up his pace, a clear sign that he was getting close.

Tameer whimpered but nodded, squeezing just a bit, pulling a pleasurable grunt from Oliver.

"Together, or not at all. Do you hear me?" Oliver pumped his hand, punctuating the words as he worked Tameer.

"Gods, yes." Tameer's voice was breathy and weak. He'd never been with someone so bossy. He'd always been the one in control. It gave him an easy out, in case things got too complicated. He already knew this was too complicated, but really didn't fucking care.

"Now. Right fucking now," Oliver grunted, his body contorting as his cock twitched in Tam's hand. At the same time, Tameer felt an explosion of pleasure start at the base of his spine before rocketing out of him, landing in a warm pool on his belly.

Oliver continued stroking him until he shuddered at the last of his release. "Gods," Tameer whispered, looking into Oliver's molten brown eyes.

Oliver smirked, placing a chaste kiss on Tameer's forehead. "Good morning indeed."

Oliver couldn't believe he'd let things get that far. In the bright light of morning, after he'd cleaned himself up and slipped into last night's clothes, he headed back to the room he shared with Matty. He'd fucked up. Not once, but multiple times in the night. Yes, obviously it had been quite the pleasurable experience, and he'd definitely needed the release, but it was a mistake.

There couldn't be anything between him and Tameer. Could there? He didn't even know if Tameer wanted that. Hells, it could have just been a good fuck for him and they'd be business as usual now. Which was to say, they'd go back to being relative strangers.

This had always been Oli's problem. He'd get too emotionally invested in people far too quickly. He was terrible at one-night-stands. He couldn't fuck someone and not feel something for them. He just wasn't built that way.

Shaking his head, Oliver tried to focus on the task at hand. Matty wanted to see the assassin today about a cure. While Oliver didn't love the idea, he sure as hells wasn't going to let Matty go alone. He needed to get his head on right so he could be useful. Coffee and a quick—cold—shower. That would fix him right up.

He opened the door to their room as quietly as possible, hoping Matty was still asleep and wouldn't notice Oliver sneaking in. He really didn't want to have the "And where were you all night?" conversation. He should have known better. His luck had never been *that* good.

"Well, good morning, sunshine. Late night?" Matty winked as he looked up from his breakfast. "I hope they were kind to you. You definitely needed a little kindness after that shitshow last night."

Oliver pulled his tunic off, throwing it at his brother who caught it with a laugh. "That good, huh?" he continued to tease. "You know, if you can't find someone to your liking, I can ask around. I know you have rather high standards, but there's bound to be someone in this town that will meet your needs."

In the wardrobe, Oliver selected the first clean shirt he could find, along with breeches, kicking off his boots and giving his beloved little brother a foul look. "Don't you fucking dare. You don't know my preferences, and I really don't want to have this conversation with you. I'm going to shower. Don't drink all the coffee. We'll head to the assassin's when I get back."

"Whatever you say, lover boy!" Matty's taunt echoed down the hall as Oliver exited their room, heading for the communal bathing rooms and some much needed alone time to think about his life choices and stew in feelings he knew he shouldn't have.

The assassin's house was easy enough to find. The scent of fresh bread and cinnamon drew them in from nearly half a mile away. Oliver had never ventured this far from the center of town, never having a need, but the house was quaint. A stone cottage with vines covering the picket fence around the property, and a stone path to the front door. He could see a glimpse of raised garden beds around the back of the house, as well as some fruit trees beyond the back fence. There were lacy curtains on the windows, making it impossible to see clearly into the house, although he suspected those inside could see out perfectly fine.

"I didn't think you'd actually come." The voice came from behind them, startling Oliver, who instantly jumped, pulling the blade from his hip and crouching as he faced the speaker.

The mountain of a man lifted his axe, resting it confidently on his shoulder as he collected an armful of logs. The look on his face was one of annoyance. He hadn't expected them to come, and he hadn't wanted them to.

"Sorry to disappoint," Matty quipped. He never did know when to keep his mouth shut.

The man, Ash, smirked. "She was right. She's always right. It's the most frustrating thing about her." Hoisting the logs a bit higher in his grasp, he stepped passed them, leading the way up to the house. "Come on then. She's been working half the night. She should be about done by now."

Oliver caught Matty's gaze, trying to impart a need to be cautious when entering the assassin's home, but Matty just smirked. His jaunty steps indicating that he wasn't remotely as concerned about this plan as he ought to be.

Ash dropped the freshly cut wood in the cast iron log holder by the entry, stomped his boots off on the stone steps, and opened the door, motioning for them to enter.

Oliver sheathed his dagger slowly, keeping a watchful eye on the big man as he hung the axe on the wall above the firewood. The second he crossed the threshold, though, Oliver felt it again. That weighty, oppressive feeling of magic. Taking in the room, Oliver saw the sparkle of it everywhere, but he couldn't seem to shake himself from its grasp.

The room shone extra bright, like the sun owed Leah a favor and offered her a spotlight with which to work as repayment. The warmth of the room was both comforting and mildly suffocating. The only thing pleasing about the entire home was the smell. Once he got passed the overwhelming scent of baked goods, herbs, and seasonings, there was a welcoming scent that was so familiar. Something soft, almost floral, with a bit of honeyed sweetness and smoke. Something Oliver couldn't help but want to curl up into and bask in for days. That smell made him feel safe and relaxed, while also lighting a fire in his blood. Why did he know that smell? Where had he experienced it before?

Turning slowly around in the room, he tried to find the source of the intoxicating aroma. The kitchen was filled with baked goods, flour covering the countertops as the assassin—and baker, it would seem—was busy working on some sort of specialized bread. Matty was stumbling over himself to try and be helpful to her. It would only be a matter of moments before Ash physically put him in a chair to get him out of the way. Oliver couldn't blame him. Leah was striking, and Matty had a hard time accepting when a woman was taken. He simply saw it as a challenge. He was going to have to learn that lesson the hard way, one of these days.

A small breeze came through the room and that scent caught Oliver's attention once more. Down the hall? Oliver didn't know what was down there, but he knew he *needed* to find out. It was the magic talking, he was certain of it, but he couldn't deny it. Something was drawing him toward that heady aroma and his body refused to ignore it. As quietly as he could manage, Oliver sidestepped the open doorway of the kitchen, down the hall to what appeared to be bedrooms. The first was empty, and in shambles. Clothing all over the floor. Male and female. Likely the room the assassin and her mountain shared. No matter. It wasn't what he was after.

A few more steps and the scent nearly knocked Oliver over it was so strong. If it was possible to get drunk on a smell, he would have been. Without thought, or even the courtesy of a knock, Oliver opened the door. Tameer was standing in the middle of the room. Breeches unlaced, no kurta. He was clearly in the middle of changing. His hair was still mussed from having tossed yesterday's clothing into the laundry basket.

He was the source of that addictive scent. Oliver immediately stepped fully into the room, closely the door firmly behind himself.

"Well, hello there. This is unexpected." Tameer's voice was a melody. A siren's song sent from the depths to draw him to his death. Oliver didn't even care. He would happily met his end worshiping this man.

He crossed the distance between them in two large strides, lacing his fingers in Tameer's hair and claiming his mouth with all the grace of a drunken sailor. Tightening his grip in Tam's hair, Oliver repositioned his head, plundering the man's mouth as though his very life depended on it. At this moment, it felt as though it did.

Tameer gasped, gripping Oliver's shoulders. Embracing the man for a split second, Tameer quickly pushed Oliver back, holding him at arm's length and studying him with an intensity Oliver couldn't help but find all the more arousing.

"Fuck," he muttered under his breath.

When Oliver moved to close the distance once more, Tameer placed a firm hand on his chest. "No. Not yet. Wait right here. I need a word with my sister."

What the fuck? Right now?

What the hells did she do?

Tameer was livid. Oliver looked high. While Tam didn't know the man that well, obviously, he didn't seem like the type to want to fuck in one room while his brother was alone with a couple of killers in another. This had Leah's magic written all over it.

"Just like that, dear. Excellent!" Leah was cooing some indulgent encouragement to her newest plaything while Ash stood stoically in the corner. Scowling. He was always scowling.

Tameer didn't bother with pleasantries. A quick nod to Ash, who could see the irritation all over Tameer's face, and Tam grabbed Leah by the arm, dragging his sister and best friend out the side door to her garden.

"Ow, hey! What the hells?" Leah struggled, but Tameer tightened his grip, not willing to have this conversation within the walls of her enchanted cottage.

"What the *fuck* did you do?" He released her when they were far enough away that their discussion wouldn't be overheard.

Leah brushed off her arm, wiping invisible wrinkles from her sleeve. "I don't know what you're talking about," she lied.

"Leah, I swear to every god under the sun and all the moon gods as well, if you lie to me one more time, I'm moving to Ravendale permanently."

That got her attention. A look of dismay flitted across her face, quickly chased away by one of indignation. "I just want you to be happy. You've been so lonely. I thought he might be a good fit for you—especially after the way the two of you went after each other in the alleyway last night. I just wanted to help things along."

Tameer began pacing along the garden boxes, flexing his hands at his sides as he debated how much to tell her.

"What? What am I missing here? I thought this was a good thing." Leah looked genuinely confused.

Tameer stopped, pivoting to face her. The look on his face must have given more away than he intended, because her expression went from confused to gleeful in seconds.

"Oh. My. GODS! You fucked him? When?! Why didn't you tell me?" Leah was practically dancing with joy at this revelation. "How was it?"

Tameer crossed to her, placing his hands on her shoulders and forcing her to calm down. Ash and Matty both looked curiously out the kitchen window. "Shut the hells up, will you? It just happened last night. Now will you please take down whatever over-the-top shit you've got on the cottage so I don't find him naked in my bed? This *really* isn't the time, Leah." As much as Tameer would love another round with Oliver, the cottage was too small and filled with far too many people at the moment.

Groaning, Leah agreed. "But you owe me details."

"Later," Tameer promised.

When they reentered the house, Leah disappeared into the living room for a few moments, wiping some runes from the archway around the windows and door. Tameer felt the shift in the house immediately. Based on the way Matty was looking at Leah, he felt it too.

"Tea, anyone? Coffee? We've also got scones, muffins, and fresh banana bread." Leah flitted around the kitchen as though nothing had happened. It was the most frustrating thing about her. Nothing ever fazed her. Tameer desperately wanted to be like that.

Oliver felt it the moment the spell was lifted. All the blood that had been rushing to his cock halted its journey before reversing course and returning to where it belonged. Dizzy, Oliver sat on the edge of Tameer's bed, resting his head in his hands and taking deep breaths to steady himself.

A gentle knock at the door drew his attention.

"You ok?" Tameer's voice was soft, concern filtering his words as he slipped in and carefully closed the door behind him.

Oliver didn't look up, ashamed and embarrassed. "Yeah," he muttered to his boots.

"I'm so sorry about all of that. Leah thought she was doing me a favor," Tameer crossed the room, kneeling in front of Oliver but not touching him. Smart. Oliver was strung as tight as a new bow. One false move and he might go off. "It will *never* happen again. I made sure of that." Tameer leaned closer, trying to angle his head to catch Oliver's gaze beneath his hands. "Are you all right? Do you want a drink? To talk? If you never want to see me again, I understand. She crossed a serious line. It was fucked up. I know I already said 'sorry' and that doesn't even begin to cover it, but fuck. Leah doesn't always think before she does things... I'm just... shit. Oliver, I'm gonna stop talking now."

Tameer sat back on his heels, patiently waiting for Oliver to respond. It was clear he'd accept whatever reaction Oliver threw at him. Unfortunately, Oliver didn't know *how* to react. He didn't know how he felt about any of it. Obviously, whatever magic Leah had done was a violation of his free will, and that pissed him the fuck off. Especially with how the Guild had been playing them for fools all these years. But she'd also unleashed some primal beast in him that Oliver had never realized he had—or perhaps had been in denial about. A beast who *craved* Tameer in the most powerful way. It had been undeniable. Even now, with the spell undone, Tameer's scent was still everywhere. His presence called to Oliver like nothing he'd ever known.

Dropping his hands, Oliver studied the man that sat before him on the stone floor. "You didn't ask her to do that." It was a statement, not a question. Tameer didn't need Leah's magic to get Oliver's attention. Not anymore.

Tameer answered all the same. "I would never." His voice was firm. Solid. Not a hint of doubt.

"Good." Oliver stood, reaching for Tameer's hand and pulling him to stand as well. Placing his hand in the middle of Tameer's chest, Oliver pushed him back against the wall, invading his space until there was nothing between them. He leaned forward, whispering his threat directly into Tam's ear. "If she ever uses that shit on me again, you'll be the one I take my frustrations out on."

8

O LIVER LEFT TAMEER TO catch his breath, striding into the kitchen as though he hadn't a care in the world. As though he hadn't just threatened endless torment—and unlimited pleasure—on the man he was originally meant to kill.

"Coffee or tea?" Leah asked, her sing-song voice annoyingly chipper after whatever cursed magic she'd wrought on him.

"Coffee," he grunted, taking a seat at the table next to his brother. Ash was leaning against the wall, glaring daggers at Matty. It seemed the two of them had not grown any friendlier in the time that Oliver had been... bonding with Tameer in the bedroom.

"Sugar? Cream? Cinnamon? Nutmeg? Ground chocolate? Turmeric? Caramel? Milk? Whipped cream?" Leah offered Oliver an extraordinarily long list of coffee additives.

"Just coffee. Thanks." He took the mug, blowing the steaming cup and eyeing her suspiciously.

"It's not poisoned, I swear! Gods, will no one trust me? I'm not going to invite you over for a cure just to kill you in my kitchen. Why would I do that?" Leah looked exasperated.

"You are known for your poisons. It would be foolish to think you hadn't at least considered it." Oliver countered, still cautious of the mug.

Sighing dramatically, Leah grabbed his mug and took a swig. "There, happy?" She handed it back as though that should settle everything.

"I might be, but I imagine any clever poisoner would build up an immunity to any of the toxins they used. To avoid accidentally killing themselves. So, no, that doesn't actually satisfy me at all."

He must've said something wrong because Leah's eyes lit up with unadulterated glee. "Oh, I know what will satisfy you."

As if on cue, Tameer entered the room.

"Tam, darling, please tell this lump of snark that I'm not trying to poison him and his coffee is safe." Leah winked at Oliver as she spoke, setting him all the more on edge. What did she know? What had he told her? It had only been a few hours. Had he already relayed all the sordid details? Fuck. Oliver wasn't sure how he felt about a highly skilled assassin knowing his secrets. He wasn't ashamed of his night with Tameer—far from it, he couldn't wait for a repeat—but since Oliver didn't know what the night meant, he wasn't sure he liked this woman knowing anything.

"I don't see why it's so odd that I would be skeptical about accepting food or drink from a known poisoner." Oliver roughed a frustrated hand over his face, hoping to drop the topic and move on to why they'd come to this damned cottage in the first place.

"Oli, please, be reasonable." Matty lifted his own cup in mock salute, taking a sip.

A wicked grin split across Tameer's teasing lips. "Oh, yes, Oli, please. Be *reasonable*."

Somehow Tameer managed to make the word sound both tantalizing and condescending. Gods, he was infuriating. Oliver had plenty of ideas for how to relieve some of his pent up frustrations, thanks to Leah's magic. But now wasn't the time. Shaking his head, he shifted in his seat, pushing the coffee aside and refocusing their conversation once and for all.

"You said you could cure my brother. Is that true or not?"

Tameer watched Oliver, smirking taking the last seat at the table—next to Oliver. He made a show of stealing Oliver's abandoned coffee and taking a long sip before placing the mug back down in front of Oliver and rising to retrieve a cup of his own. Internally groaning, Oliver accepted the mug at last and took a tentative sip. It was delicious. Dammit.

A teasing grin tugged at Leah's lips as she watched the interaction before responding. "Yeah, I can do it. I checked through my books last night. I've got everything I need here in my garden, except the crocette mushroom, but the witch healer should have some at the market today. I'll brew it up with the moon tonight and have it ready by week's end."

Oliver sat back in the chair, stunned. A cure by week's end. It was hard to imagine a world in which his brother wasn't sick.

Their lives had revolved around Matty's sickness and working for the Guild in exchange for medicine for so long. Oliver couldn't picture what it would be like to live without that weight dragging him down. It was surreal.

"What about the Guild?" Matty asked. "They expect us to kill Tameer. If we don't do it, won't they just send someone else?"

Leah pulled two wicked, curved blades from sheaths at the base of her spine, twirling them between her fingers with practiced ease. "Let them try."

The market was thriving by the time they arrived. Tameer trailed behind Oliver and Matty, with Ash a step behind him. Leah led their little troupe through town, confidently spinning her karambit knives in the afternoon sun. It was a clear sign to any watching that she was on her guard and not afraid to spill the blood of anyone foolish enough to attack them.

Plus, she really liked showing off her knife skills.

"You like him, huh?" Ash kept his voice quiet so it didn't carry, but the bluntness of his question still shocked Tameer. They weren't exactly close, but they'd bonded enough over one too many drinks and childhood trauma. Tameer considered Ash to be a friend, if a bit quiet and standoffish at times.

He debated feigning ignorance, but ultimately decided it wasn't worth the effort. Anything Tam told Leah would likely be shared with Ash by the end of the night. No point in denying it. "He's interesting. And easy on the eyes."

"I told Leah that spell was a shit idea. But you know how she is. Once she gets an idea in her head, she won't be talked out of it." It was Ash's version of an apology.

Nodding, Tameer grinned. "Like that time she decided to help you kill the king?"

A grunt of amusement escaped Ash's lips. "Exactly."

The witch seemed to be waiting for them as they approached her stand. She always seemed to know things before they happened. It irked Tam to no end. If she had that sort of insight, why not share the intel? Sure, the town was filled with criminals, murderers, and thieves, but there was a code, dammit! She should adhere to it like the rest of them. Using her skills to the benefit of all and only harming her neighbors if it's unavoidable.

"Took y'all long enough," she chastised, gnarled hands on hips. "I expected y'all here twenty minutes ago."

"So sorry to keep you waiting, Mama Orenda. If only we'd known we had an appointment with you, we would have been on time." Tameer couldn't keep the snark from his tone, not that he tried.

"Don't get smart with me, boy. I have half a mind to send you home with nothing but your dick in your hands and a bruise on your cheek for that sass." Mama never did hold back.

"Mama." Leah stepped in before Tameer could come back with another snide retort. "We could really use your help. As I'm sure you know, these boys have been lied to for quite some time. This young man"—she shoved Matheu forward—"has been living with red lung for years, surviving with some medicinal treatments regularly, rather than being given the cure. I was hoping you'd have some crocette mushrooms on hand—that I could purchase for a fair price—to finish the cure for him and finally free him from this awful disease."

Mama Orenda glared at Tameer for a second longer before turning her focus to Matheu. Her eyes wandered slowly up and down, taking him in. Nodding, she seemed to accept the truth of Leah's words. She might be the most skilled assassin in Mistfall—arguably the world—but Leah also had a silver tongue and knew how to talk her way into or out of whatever she needed. And it helped that Mama liked her. They traded gardening tips regularly. And Leah had never once vomited in her prized rose bushes. Tameer couldn't say the same.

"I've got a bundle waiting for you. Two silvers and they're yours, darlin'." Mama's tone with Leah was always so much sweeter than anything she used with Tameer. It grated, but he held his tongue. Whatever it took to get Oliver out from under the Guild's thumb.

Leah pressed three silver coins into the older woman's wrinkled hand, accepting the bundle of mushrooms in returning. "Goddess bless you. You're a literal lifesaver, Mama."

Tameer wasn't positive, but he thought he saw a blush creep up the old witch's leathery face. He hadn't thought that harpy was capable of such emotions. He kept his bemusement to himself as they turned and headed back to the cottage. Maybe the witch had a heart after all.

Leah had assured them that the cure would be finished by the end of the week. The twins would be back in a few days for confirmation that Oliver had completed the job. They would be cutting it close, to say the least. It had Oliver on edge, and apparently, he was taking it out on the food.

"Get yer head outta yer ass, boy. This soup tastes like hot garbage. What the hells are ye doing in there?" Geoffree tossed the bowl back at Oliver through the small window between the bar and the kitchen.

Fuck. Oliver honestly wasn't paying attention. He had no idea what he'd put in the soup pot. Grunting, he removed the steaming cauldron from the hook over the fire and dumped the contents into the drain that led to the alley and ultimately to the sewer system. Time to start over, he supposed.

Using the water pump, he refilled the cauldron before hooking it back over the cooking fire.

"I'm heading to the storeroom. Fresh supplies. New soup. Maybe you'll bitch less this time." Oliver wasn't sure why he bothered telling Geoffree where he was going, the old man didn't give two shits, but he always felt compelled to keep the man informed.

In case the Guild decided he was taking too long on a task and sent a hitter again, Oliver thought. It was self preservation.

He needed someone to know where he was, so he wouldn't be caught alone and unaware again.

Oliver dug around the stores of produce, picking out potatoes, onions, carrots, radishes, and celery. He had the meat and herbs he'd need upstairs. Loading up the basket of produce for the evening meal, he froze.

Was that a shuffle of feet? Or was he just being paranoid? Holding his breath, Oliver was as still as a statue as he listened intently. No, someone else was definitely down there with him. Not Geoffree. That man had no stealth. He owned the place and walked as loudly as he pleased. No, this person was light on their feet, and not entirely sure of their whereabouts.

Oliver crouched low, slipping behind a barrel of apples, watching from the shadows, his dagger in hand. Whoever was coming for him wasn't going to catch him ill-prepared.

Seconds dragged on. Oliver's heart pounded so loudly he was certain his stalker would hear it and find him with ease. And then a figure stepped into the light. A very familiar figure. One Oliver couldn't wait to sink his teeth into.

Debating his options, a wicked grin split across Oliver's face. If Tameer came here to surprise him, he was going to get the shock of his life.

Sinking deeper into the shadows, Oliver tracked Tam's movements, watching his eyes flit around the room. He was looking for Oliver. Too bad Tam wouldn't see him coming. The second Tameer crossed in front of Oliver, he sprang into action.

Grabbing ahold of the ex-thief, Oliver wrapped an arm around the man's middle, pressing his body firmly against his chest. Raising his dagger slowly, Oliver traced Tameer's racing heartbeat along his neck with the barest touch of the blade.

"Stalking me, eh?" Oliver said in a harsh whisper, his voice a warm breath on the shell of Tameer's ear. Oliver felt the shiver that ran down the length of Tam's body. It was absolutely delicious. Oliver's body reacted immediately.

It took Tam a moment to catch his breath, a glorious moment in which Oliver basked in the scent of the man's musk as his arousal became evident. As if on instinct, Tameer pushed back against Oliver, drawing an illicit groan from the dagger-wielding man. "I was actually here to see if you needed help." Tameer's voice was rough and intoxicating.

Oliver sheathed his dagger and returned his grip to Tameer's throat in one fluid motion. Grasping his neck, he squeezed just enough to command Tam's full attention. "I know how you can help me." Oliver ground his cock into the man's ass, making his intentions known. A pleading whimper escaped Tameer's lips as he leaned back, tilting his head and resting it on Oliver's shoulder.

Oliver used his grip on Tam's throat to turn his head, claiming his lips and plundering his mouth as though his life depended on it. Tameer answered in kind.

Gasping, they separated for a moment, foreheads pressed together as they struggled to catch their breath. Tameer sighed into Oliver, reaching back to run his fingers through Oliver's now-mussed hair. He tugged teasingly, chuckling at Oliver's groaning response. That touch shredded the last thread of restraint Oliver had.

The arm around Tameer's middle pulled tight, erasing what little distance had been between them, as the hand around Tam's throat tightened.

"Drop your pants," Oliver growled.

9

B Y THE END OF the week, Oliver thought he might peel his own skin off if he didn't hear from Leah. Somehow, they'd managed to avoid contact with the twins, but they were rapidly running out of time. The Guild would expect confirmation of the job's completion soon.

Oliver was trying to ignore the way his brother anxiously cleaned his nails with a small knife at the end of the bar when Tameer sauntered in. Nearly launching himself over the bar, Oliver reached Tameer in record time.

"Does she have it? Is it finished?"

"Well, it's lovely to see you as well, Oli. Nice night we're having, eh? The weather has been quite warm of late, but this breezy evening is just what the witch doctor ordered, am I right?" Tameer grinned like a fool, hands shoved in his pockets with the confident air of someone who wasn't being hunted by the Thieves' Guild. Again.

"Tam, please. I'm going crazy here. Just tell me what's going on." Oliver couldn't keep the pleading note from his words.

"Oooh, begging. I like you begging. Do it again." A husky rasp coated Tam's voice, shifting the tension between them.

"Please," Oliver offered placatingly.

The gleam of power in Tameer's eyes was intoxicating. If the moment wasn't so charged with stress, Oliver might have thrown the man over his shoulder and taken him back to the storeroom for another round.

"Please, Tameer, just put us out of our misery. I need to know if I should start drinking now in celebration or sorrow." Matty's voice killed the unexpected heat that had been building between Tam and Oliver, dumping a bucket of ice water on their collective dirty minds.

Tameer gave Oliver a look that simply said *Later*, and focused on Matty. "It's done. Leah would like you to come over, so she can give you the proper dose. She also requested—against Ash's better judgment—that you stay overnight, in case you have any adverse reactions."

Oliver grabbed Matty's arm, halting his little brother's progress as the man immediately tried to bolt for the door. "What sort of 'adverse reactions' are we talking about?"

Tameer shrugged. "Leah can explain." Then he turned on his heel and led them from the tavern.

"Nausea. Heartburn. Indigestion. Upset stomach. Diarrhea. Vomiting. Fever. Chills. Headache. Migraine. A ringing in the ears. You know, all the standard things." Leah was very nonchalant about the list of potential side effects. Oliver couldn't wrap his mind around it.

"Hells, your side effects sound worse than his actual symptoms!" Roughing a hand over the three-day scruff that had taken up residence on his tired face, Oliver paced the room. The anxiety over the veracity of the assassin and her supposed cure coupled with the unexpected... coupling with Tameer had left little time for frivolous things like daily shaving.

Leah raised an incredulous eyebrow at Oliver, hand on hip as she stared him down. Despite her diminutive stature, she held a commanding presence. "Considering the actual symptoms, when left untreated, lead to *death*, I think this is a considerable improvement." She turned to Matty, effectively dismissing Oliver which irritated him to no end. "Darling, it's your choice. It's your body. If you want the cure, I've got it. You're welcome to spend the night here, to make sure none of the side effects get unbearable. By morning, you should be free and clear. No more red lung and no more Guild."

Oliver knew what Matty would choose before she even finished her speech. Matty blamed himself for everything their family had been through since he'd gotten sick. Every job they'd ever been forced to take from the Guild. Every time they'd risked their lives to get his medicine. He would do anything to get them out from under the Guild's control. Side effects be damned.

Matty took the proffered, softly glowing, bottle of red liquid. Pulling the cork from the bottle, he downed the entire bottle in one go.

"Well, that settles that, I guess. Good thing it was all one dose," Leah teased. "Too much and you'd be spending the night with your head in a bucket, praying for death."

Matty had the decency to look mildly sheepish, but that shit-eating grin never quite left his cocky face. "Now what?" he asked, replacing the cork and handing the empty bottle back to the assassin.

"Now, we wait." She motioned for him to move to the den. "Best go lie down. From what I've heard, the effects can kick in rather quickly. You've been infected longer than most. I imagine we're in for a rough night. You've got a lot to expel... Sorry, darlin'. But by morning, you should be feeling all shiny and new!"

Should be being the operative phrase.

Leah was annoyingly right. Within minutes of Matty entering the den, Oliver heard the coughing and retching of his little brother as the cure began its work. Expelling the taint the red lung had wrought on his brother all these years.

It was going to be a very rough night indeed.

Tameer had never considered himself a weak-stomached individual, but with every heave of Matheu's intestines, Tam felt a gag at the base of his own throat threaten. Leah and Ash had long since abandoned the brothers to their turmoil. She'd left a collection of various medicines, compresses, ointments, and teas to ease Matheu's suffering, but they'd quickly learned that Ash—despite his very manly appearance—had no tolerance for the scent of another man's vomit. At Matheu's first hurl, Ash had rushed outside to evacuate his own stomach's contents in the bushes.

Leah had rolled her eyes at his antics, but followed after him. When it was clear Ash wouldn't be able to be in the same house as Matheu overnight, Tameer had given them the key to his room at the inn and Leah had handed him an exceedingly long list of information for each medication, dosage, and instructions for proper usage.

Oliver spent the night on the floor beside the couch, placing fresh compresses on his brother's placid forehead and occasionally dumping the bucket before replacing it near his brother's head. In the beginning, his vomit had been a *very* alarming, vibrant shade of red. Leah had warned them that would be the case. It wasn't blood. She'd been very clear about that. Red lung was aptly named, in that it coated one's lungs with a sticky red substance that, over time, made breathing very difficult. As the night progressed, the scarlet color faded until he was coughing up clear phlegm by morning light. It was considerably less disgusting, thank the gods.

As the sun shone through the kitchen window, Tameer set about boiling water for coffee and tea, leaving Oliver to sleep as comfortably as he could—half curled on the floor with Matheu passed out, drooling on the couch.

Mindlessly setting about his morning routine, Tameer's thoughts wandered. It was strange to think that just two weeks prior, he'd been in the castle with Irena, spending his mornings with the little prince, filling his time and desperately trying to ignore the ache of loneliness that was growing stronger every day. Now, here he was, making coffee for a man who'd first tried to kill him—very badly, he might add—and then fucked him *very* well multiple times over the last few days. Tam didn't like to worry about the future, but he couldn't help wondering what would happen next. Now that Matheu was cured, the brothers wouldn't be working for the Guild anymore, which meant they could go wherever they wanted. Do whatever they wanted. They weren't tied to this town anymore. A sudden, unwelcomed sadness settled in Tameer's chest at the thought of Oliver leaving. He didn't know how he felt about the man—obviously they'd just met and he had no real ties to him, other than knowing he was a *very* good fuck—but he wasn't ready to watch him leave. Not yet.

Hearing movement in the den, Tameer shook the thoughts from his mind. It wasn't his decision anyway. Oliver didn't owe him anything. They had fun together. That's all it was.

The kettle began to sing just as Oliver shuffled into the room.

"Perfect timing," Tameer sang, forcing more cheer into his voice than he felt. "Tea or coffee?"

Oliver wiped sleep from his eyes, practically collapsing into a chair at the small dining table. "Coffee. All the coffee, please."

Tameer set a steaming cup in front of him, as well as a small tray of scones and cinnamon rolls and Leah's "Coffee fixin's" collection. That half-fae woman liked her coffee to taste more like overly sweetened syrup with a dash of caffeine. Tameer smiled at the thought. He did miss mornings with his sister. Not enough to make him come back and listen to her nights with Ash, but enough to make him consider breakfast with her on a regular basis.

"Did you get any sleep last night?" Tameer asked, pouring himself a cup of coffee and dropping a dallop of cream into it, along with a dash of cinnamon. Stirring slowly, he studied Oliver's exhausted face. The dark circles under the man's eyes were answer enough, but he waited for Oli's response all the same.

Shrugging, Oliver took a long pull from his coffee, closing his eyes and savoring the flavor. "About as much as he did, I suspect."

"You'll both need a few days to recover. Once he's up and mobile, I can help you move him to my bed. You can both sleep here, if you'd like. Proper sleep. I'll take the couch. Unless you'd prefer to get back to your room at the inn. In which case, I'll help you get him back there." *And I can get my key back from Leah*, Tameer thought.

Oliver stared unseeingly into his coffee, his mind clearly elsewhere. Tameer gently reached across the table, placing a hand over Oliver's in an attempt to bring him back to earth. "You ok?"

Shaking his head, Oliver refocused on the room around him. "Sorry, what? Yeah, no, I'm okay. Just tired, I guess. The inn. The inn would be good. Back in his own bed. It will be less confusing for him to wake up somewhere he knows." Oliver blinked a few times, taking another long drink of his coffee, downing the rest of the cup. "Plus, he keeps hitting on your sister. I'd hate for her to cure him, just for her mate to have to kill him." There was that twinkle of humor in his eyes again.

Relief flowed through Tameer. He'd started to worry that Oliver was pulling away. Creating distance for reasons Tameer wasn't privy to. This little jab, though, was the Oliver Tameer knew and loved.

No. Not *love*. He barely knew the man. He couldn't possibly love him.

That would be ludicrous.

10

I T HAD TAKEN QUITE a bit of effort to damn-near carry Matty back to their room at the inn, but Oliver needed to get them back. The closeness of Tameer... the ever present smell of him... the feel of his eyes always watching... it was overwhelming. Oliver needed to clear his mind. He needed space to figure out their next steps.

His family had been shackled by Matty's sickness for so long, chained by the Guild for years. Oliver truly didn't know what their life would be like without that weight constantly pulling them down.

Their parents were still locked away. A problem that he could now pour all of his focus into solving. Well, once Matty was awake again. Matheu had a quick mind, when he wasn't getting distracted by pretty pink-haired fae who were clearly taken and so obviously out of his league. After a good, long rest, he and Matty would come up with a plan to free their parents from that merchant's less-than-legal dungeon. Then they'd go after the Guild. Or run.

But Tameer.

Running meant leaving Tameer. The thought alone felt like someone had an icy vice-like grip around Oliver's chest. He might not have known the man for very long, but the thought of abandoning him was unacceptable. Unbearable. In the few days they'd spent together, Tameer had worked his way under Oliver's skin and burrowed into his heart and mind. It was unsettling, and yet it felt right. As though Tameer was the missing piece he'd been searching for all this time. Gods, he was a fool.

Matty snorted in his sleep, rolling over in the bed, momentarily shaking Oliver out of his reverie. His brother was well, or would be soon enough. That's where his focus needed to be. Not on some man he barely knew. His family needed him now more than ever. Oliver didn't have time for extraneous attachments.

"Ye got visitors." Geoffree rapped his knuckles on the counter between the kitchen and the bar.

Looking up from the night's stew, Oliver saw the twins stride into the bar, taking up residence at one of the booths along the wall. His gaze flicked momentarily to Geoffree. Oliver didn't know how much the man knew about Oliver's family business, but as a retired hitter, the man knew a great deal about Mistfall's underworld. Not to mention, he seemed to have earned Tameer and Leah's trust. Hells, for all Oliver knew, Geoffree was better informed than him at this point.

Nodding, Oliver wiped his hands on his apron before untying the garment and tossing it onto the counter. He still hadn't worked out what he was going to say to the twins or the Guild. Every time he thought about it, Oliver's rage boiled over. He couldn't think straight, much less clever-tongue his way out of this situation. He'd been relying on Matty for that, but his brother was still passed out from exhaustion. Expelling years worth of red lung would do that, apparently.

Oliver wracked his brain for something—anything—to say as he crossed the tavern. He slid into the booth across from the twins while Eva studied him intently.

"Well?" she prompted, impatience sharpening the word.

Oliver swiped her tankard of ale, taking a confident swig in an attempt to buy himself a few precious seconds while he desperately tried to come up with something witty to say.

He was spared—or damned—when a pink-haired woman slipped in the booth beside him, her mountain of a man posting up as a blockade, pinning Evan and Eva in.

"Good evening, lovelies," Leah cooed. Oliver tried to sense her magic, but was surprised when he felt nothing. Instead, the assassin pulled out her wicked blades—karambits, Tameer had called them—and began flipping them expertly between her fingers. Tameer strode confidently into the tavern, commanding every eye as though he were the godsdamn king.

Eva's eyes filled with rage, pinning Oliver with a glare he was sure would have made him shudder two weeks ago, but now just made him grin. Evan, on the other hand, was in awe of Tameer. Mouth hung open like a fool, he stared at the man with unabashed admiration. Oliver wanted to slap the expression off the messenger's face. Tameer was *his*. No other man had the right to stare at him so openly.

What the fuck? Oliver thought. *Where the hells did that come from?*

Shaking the feeling, Oliver focused on the scene as it played out before him.

Tameer pulled up a seat from a neighboring table, placing himself at the head of theirs as he studied Eva and Evan. He seemed to be assessing them before making it clear that he found them lacking.

"So these are the two ravens the Guild sent, eh? I'm offended. I would have thought the Guild would send more worthy opponents to deal with the likes of me." Tameer stretched back in his chair, casually throwing an arm over the back of it as he rested one ankle on his knee.

Oliver couldn't help but feel drawn to the man in this state. This was the Tameer who'd led the Thieves' Guild for so many years. *This* man exuded power from every pore. It was intoxicating. Oliver's mind was drifting to the things he would do to feel that power, feel Tameer give into him. It was all the more intoxicating to see him in this position of authority and then have him on his knees, begging for more.

Tam, somehow sensing where Oliver's mind had gone, caught his eye and with a subtle wink, promised so much more.

Fuck. Focus! Oliver took another pull from Eva's ale, glorying in her scowl as it deepened.

"You're really him, aren't you? Gods, it's an honor to meet you, sir." Evan was practically drooling, tripping over himself in his excitement at meeting Tameer.

"An honor?" Tameer's eyebrow shot up so high it disappeared beyond his dark lock. "An honor to meet the man you blackmailed this man into attempting to kill?" He gestured to Oliver as he spoke. There was an edge to his voice—something like rage, but with a hint of passion that set the hairs on Oliver's neck on end.

Evan stumbled on his words, struggling to put together a coherent thought, or even a legitimate word. Eva stepped in, saving her twin from himself. "We were following orders."

"Ah, yes, the age old excuse." Tameer turned to Ash. "Isn't that what the guards said when they killed your mother and tried to kill you?"

Ash ground his teeth, glaring daggers at the twins with a single nod.

"And isn't that the same excuse your trainer used when he raped you, Leah?"

"Not quite." Leah stabbed the table with one of her karambits and used the other to clean nonexistent dirt from under her nails. "He said it was common practice though. Raping was a regular punishment for girls who couldn't follow direction. I'm sure you know all about that, don't you, Eva, dear?"

Eva flinched at Leah's words. Evan's face turned rage-full. It was true. Women in the Guild were treated with especially harsh punishments, simply because of their gender. Men felt entitled to use their bodies as they saw fit. The women were supposed to accept it if they wanted to stay alive and in the Guild.

Supposedly, under Tam's leadership, such practices had been banned, but Oliver hadn't been around during that time and it seemed Eva hadn't either.

"That's just the way things are," Eva finally gritted out.

"And that makes it okay, does it?" Leah countered.

They sat in silence for several long moments.

Evan sighed, caving under the weight of the awkward stillness. "What do you propose?"

"Well, I wanted to kill you both?" Leah replied with a sinister grin, freeing her blade from the table and twirling both karambits again.

Evan and Eva flinched, leaning back in their booth.

Tameer sat forward, raising his hands placatingly. "I declined that offer," he said quickly. "Oliver thought you were both fairly reasonable people and might be open to a different arrangement."

Oliver tried to school his face. *What the hells was Tameer talking about? What arrangement?* He'd never talked to Tam about the twins at all.

"I was thinking," Tam began, looking pointedly at Oliver. "That we should go have a chat with the leader of the Guild to settle all of this. Once and for all."

Oh, fuck. This was a terrible *idea.*

"That's your plan? You want to go *talk* to them?"

Tameer understood why Oliver was upset, but he hadn't expected him to be so outraged. Shit. It was a good plan. Well, it was a half decent plan, at least. Better than any of the others Leah and Ash had thrown out the night before.

Most of which included a great deal of murder and bloodshed.

Tameer wasn't opposed to bloodshed, but as an ultimate last resort. Not a first choice.

"It's not the best idea I've ever had, sure, but it's the best one we could come up with on the fly that didn't involve a lot of violence." Tameer cocked an eyebrow at Oliver from across the storeroom. "Unless you've suddenly changed your mind about killing folks?"

The glare Oliver leveled at him was answer enough, and really fucking hot. Tameer's mind flashed back to the last time they'd been alone in this storeroom. They'd been having a very different—although equally passionate—exchange.

"I don't like the idea of you, of *anyone*, putting themselves in danger for me and my family." Oliver's words were clipped.

Tam got the feeling that the man was trying to create some distance, put up walls. It was an instinct Tameer understood, but in this moment, he hated it.

"With all due respect, my would-be killer, the Guild blackmailed *you* into killing *me*. If anything, I'm just going to the source and dealing with a threat to my life. It just so happens that the threat is highly attractive and gets the most adorable line between his brows when he's irritated. Yes! Right there!" Tameer brushed his thumb against the aforementioned line. He understood the walls Oliver was attempting to build, but it didn't mean he had to accept them. Besides, there was no reason to think this "relationship" would go much farther. Tam wanted to enjoy it for as long as he possibly could.

Oliver grunted, but didn't pull away as Tameer closed the remainder of the distance between them. Wrapping an arm around the man's neck, Tameer locked eyes with him. "If you don't want to come with us, I understand. You and Matheu are free from your shackles. If you want to run, liberate your parents and never look back, I completely understand and won't hold anything against you."

Something flashed in Oliver's eyes. Disappointment? Anxiety? Whatever it was, it was gone in a blink. Tameer tried to ignore it. Oliver was under no obligations to him. They were two men who just happened to enjoy fucking each other. Nothing more.

"Of course I'm going with you," Oliver said, a steely edge of resolve in his voice. "I'm not letting you into that viper's nest without me." His hands settled on Tameer's waist, fingers digging into the flesh in an almost-bruising, possessive grasp.

Tameer wasn't sure what to think of this sudden shift in Oliver's temperament, but the fire in the man's eyes left no room for argument. Pressing his forehead to Oliver's, Tameer closed his eyes for a second, taking a deep breath and savoring the moment.

"It's going to be fine," he whispered. "The Guild just needs a reminder of who I am and why they should leave me the fuck alone. Then we can get back to our lives."

Whatever that may look like, Tameer wasn't sure, but he desperately hoped it would include more moments like this with this man.

11

Tameer was insane. There was no other word for it, but gods damn him, Oliver was *not* letting him wander into the Guild's headquarters alone.

Granted, Leah and Ash would be with him. Leah was a trained assassin. The best in the world, bar none. That didn't matter. Oliver refused to let Tameer out of his sight. That man was so stubborn and irrationally overconfident. He was convinced he could talk himself out of any situation.

Unfortunately, life had proven Tameer right time and again, but his luck was bound to run out, and Oliver was going to be at that man's side at all times. If for no other reason than to ensure his safety amongst the two-face, silver-tongued devils that lived in the Guild's halls.

"You seem distracted." Matty laced his boots while eying his brother with a mixture of curiosity and concern.

"I don't like this plan. Just walking in there like they own the place? It's arrogant and foolhardy." Oliver roughed a hand over his face. The scruff on his face had quickly grown into a full beard. He'd been meaning to shave for days, but Tameer seemed to like it. The man was always toying with the hair...

Focus! Oliver chided.

"Well, didn't they? At least, Tameer did at one point, right? And for a while. He ran the Guild for nearly a decade, according to Evan."

That caught Oliver's full attention. "When the hells were you talking to Evan?" There was an accusatory tone to Oliver's words that he hadn't intended, but he didn't take back. His brother shouldn't be alone with the twins. They were not to be trusted.

"Last night. When you and Tameer disappeared into the storeroom," he said pointedly. "Leah, Ash, and Eva were discussing various weapons. Evan and I got to chatting about the Guild. Evan seemed to think that not everyone was so unhappy about Tameer's reign as leader. In fact, he thought a lot of the younger members would welcome him back with open arms."

Well, that was an interesting twist. Oliver wasn't sure what he'd been expecting, but it wasn't that.

"Evan mentioned that a lot of the members who'd pushed for Tameer's removal had either retired, been imprisoned, or killed. Only a handful remain active in the Guild these days." Matty continued, oblivious to the shift in Oliver's attitude. "I'd be willing to bet, the majority of the Guild will be thrilled to see him. The changes he was trying to make—banning child labor, rape and other violence as punishment—were welcome changes for the younger members, but it was the older members that fought against it. They were sick fucks who liked the power they could wield over those who were smaller than them. Even their own apprentices. Tameer's changes would probably be well received now."

Oliver's mind was whirling like the gears of a dwarven machine. If what Matty said was true, and Evan was right, maybe Tameer's plan was even better than he knew.

Something akin to optimism bolstered through Oliver's chest.

The Thieves' Guild had made their base on the edge of the merchant's quarter of Ravendale, along the river that led out of the capital and to the sea. It was a convenient location for shipping, stealing, escaping, and hiding out. Plus and easy boat ride to and from Vexia if one was so inclined.

The Guild had taken over an entire warehouse during Tameer's tenure as leader, and it seemed they hadn't improved on the space much since his abrupt departure. From the outside, one might suspect the buildings to be abandoned, rather than the headquarters of the illustrious Thieves' Guild.

While an argument could be made that inconspicuousness was a thief's bread and butter, Tameer always prided himself on his appearance. He preferred the "hiding in plain sight" technique instead. When he ran the Guild, not only had they run multiple thieving operations daily, but they'd had a thriving *legal* trade business as well. They'd had three store fronts, selling various items—sometimes even repurposed items they'd nicked on the streets and selling them back to their original owners! It was quite the scam. Not to mention, it was a safe place for the members who didn't want to be—or were terrible—thieves, but needed work to earn their keep.

Tameer wasn't surprised that the Guild had quickly killed that branch of his legacy. Didn't mean it didn't hurt though.

From the roof of an abandoned warehouse across the street, Tameer sat in the shadows with Leah, watching the comings and goings at the entrance to the Guild's not-so-secret headquarters.

"Gods, they really let the place go to shit, huh?" Leah mutter, as a shingle slid off the roof of the warehouse serving as the Guild's home.

"It's depressing, honestly. Do you remember the way it use to shine at night? The lights in the upper floors would glow through the crystal windows, lighting up the whole block. It felt like a home back then. Now it looks like a place you go to get murdered by angry poltergeists." Tameer sighed, leaning back against the rusted aluminum siding. How could they have ruined all the good he'd done so quickly? It was as though they'd gone out of their way to tear down any improvements he'd made. To erase his changes and revert back to the way they'd been before he'd taken over.

Had they truly hated his leadership so much?

"What are we doing here, Tam?" Leah asked. Curiosity with just a hint of concern in her voice. Why *were* they there? It was clear the Guild didn't want Tameer around. Why was he bothering to attempt a peaceful conclusion when they'd chosen violence at every turn? He should just let Leah have her way, cut the head off the snake and send a clear message that he should be left alone.

Pulling his knees up to his chest, Tameer wrapped his arms around them and buried his head in the space between. "I have no idea," he replied, his voice muffled.

Tameer had been so optimistic when he'd taken over the Guild. He'd been the youngest leader the Guild had ever had, and he'd had *big* plans for making dramatic changes that he'd thought would improve the lives of all members. With Leah at his side, he'd begun to initiate said changes, with minimal pushback. No one wanted to risk being on the receiving end of one of Leah's karambits or her designer poisons. But when she went off to find herself as a baker, things had gone down hill very quickly. Maybe Leah's presence was the only thing that had been keeping Tameer in power. Perhaps the Guild hadn't been as thrilled by Tameer's leadership as he'd thought. He knew the older members hadn't appreciated his changes, but he'd thought he was winning over the newer and younger members.

Gods, Tameer used to be so confident. Now, though, he was starting to see that perhaps he'd just been arrogant.

Leah nudged his shoulder, nearly knocking him out of his ball-shape. "Talk to me."

"What if this was all a waste of time?"

"What do you mean?"

Sighing, Tameer uncoiled himself, stretching his legs and staring out at the stars in the cloudless night sky. "What if you were right and we should have just sent a brute force message? Some severed, bloody heads or whatever. The Guild clearly didn't like the way I was running things. They reverted back to their old ways as soon as I was gone."

"What the hells are you talking about?" Leah looked genuinely baffled by Tameer's logic.

Tameer gestured to the decrepit warehouse across the street as though it were proof enough.

"Tam, just because some old fucks decided they didn't like change and tried to have you killed doesn't mean you were wrong. Hells, if anything, you should take it as confirmation that you were right."

Tameer scoffed. "Of course you'd think that. Normal people don't take attempts on their life as a compliment, Leah."

Rolling her eyes, Leah bumped Tameer with her shoulder before resting her head on his. "Since when have either of us ever been considered normal? Why would we ever want to be?"

Conceding her point, Tameer let his mind drift on the late night breeze. The Guild's headquarters was situated just west of Ravendale. It had taken them the better part of the day to walk here from Vexia, but they hadn't been in a hurry. No reason to rush in, now that Matheu was healed and their plan was rather basic.

A chat. A simple, direct conversation.

With the people who wanted him dead.
Many times over.
This should be fun.

12

TAMEER HAD TRIED TO convince Oliver to stay with Matheu, who was still occasionally coughing up a color, but Oliver was nothing if not stubborn. The argument was settled when Oliver grabbed Tameer by the collar, pushed him against the wall and whispered into his ear, "I go where you go."

It was both a threat and the hottest statement anyone had ever said to him. Tameer was instantly puddy in the man's hands. It was some of the most intoxicating sex they'd had yet. Who was Tameer to argue with such a sentiment?

Still, as they stood before the dilapidated door, Tam started to worry that he'd made the wrong decision. Again. Letting people in was a sure way to get them killed. It was a miracle that Leah hadn't been murdered yet.

Looking over at his best friend and adopted sister, Tameer felt a smile tug at his lips. She was far too stubborn to die. Not to mention the mountain of a man to her right would burn the world to the ground before he let anything happen to her. He'd proven that time and again. Feeling his gaze on her, Leah looked up and gave Tam a cocky wink. It was time.

Taking a deep, fortifying breath, Tameer reached for the door.

Adrenaline coursed through Oliver's body, his heart racing like he'd just run a marathon rather than merely having crossed a threshold. He'd only stepped foot in the Guild's headquarters a handful of times over the course of their tenure as indentured servants, and it always shocked him. The level of disarray and utter filth that they lived in was appalling. Oliver was used to living on the move, never staying in one place too long, so he'd always assumed when someone settled down, they'd make that place a *home*. The warehouse was anything but. Piles of literal garbage greeted them upon entry to the building, along with the overwhelming smell of human waste and body odor. Oliver immediately felt sick.

"Gods, what have they done to this place?" Disgust and pity filled Tameer's voice as he took in the view. His gaze never settled on any one spot for too long, flicking all over the expanse with a growing look of horror.

"Fuck," Leah exhaled, removing her scarf from her neck and quickly retying it around her mouth and nose. "This is fucking *disgusting*."

A rat scurried across their path, causing Ash to jump back, drawing his weapon on instinct. A giggle bubbled up Leah's throat, which promptly earned her a glare. Oliver thought he heard Ash threaten something about punishing her for that later, but he didn't have a chance to read into those words. A group of rather unfriendly looking folks were coming to greet them, wickedly sharp weapons in hand.

"What 'ave we got 'ere?" A balding man who looked to be in his late twenties picked his teeth with his blade as he eyed them with arrogant derision.

"Take me to your leader." Tameer's voice was confident. Commanding. He gave Oliver a sly grin. Winking, he added, "I've always wanted to say that."

"Why the hells would we do that?" An oily, short man demanded. He stepped up, puffing his chest as though he could intimidate them into backing off.

Ash moved to meet the man, but Tameer gave a subtle shake of his head. Leah placed a staying hand on Ash's arm, halting his progress in an instant.

Tameer took a single step forward, placing himself ahead of their troupe and instantly raising Oliver's blood pressure. "I want to look into the eyes of the people who keep trying to have me killed."

The welcoming committee stared blankly at them for several painfully long seconds before Tameer's words finally sank into their thick skulls. It was apparent when realization finally dawned on their dim faces. Eyes growing wide, mouths hanging open.

"Nah," one of them finally said. The balding one. "Ye ain't 'im. 'E's bigger than ye. Yer a scrawny li'l thing."

Leah's guffaw echoed through the ramshackle warehouse. Tameer's glare could have melted glass.

Turning back to address the group with blades still half-assedly trained on them, Tameer tried again. "I'm here to speak with your boss. Where can I find them?"

Oliver watched the group warily. They seemed to be debating their options. Whispering amongst themselves, an emaciated woman appeared to be in charge of their troupe. Pointing angrily at them, the woman hissed something to the others before two of the men disappeared back down the hall they'd entered through. Decision seemingly made, she faced them.

"We'll take you to the boss, but only you. The rest of ye stay here." Her voice was raspy, like it didn't get much use. Or perhaps she'd spent far too long screaming. Oliver truly hoped it was the former.

Tameer stepped forward, readily accepting the woman's terms without a counter. Hells no. Oliver grabbed Tameer's sleeve, pulling him backward. Catching his eyes, he reminded that damned man of their agreement. *I go where you go.*

"Oh, right. I accept on one condition: he comes too." Tameer countered, not taking his eyes off Oliver, a spark of heat in his amber eyes.

Grumbling met his response, but the woman conceded with an annoyed nod.

Leah caught Tameer's arm.

"Don't do anything stupid." she whispered keeping her eyes on the woman across the way. "You said talk. If I hear a single grunt, I'm coming in there with *all* my blades, do you hear me?"

"Yes, ma'am," Tameer said with a patronizing smile. He patted her hand, then pressed a quick kiss to her temple. Giving a small nod to Ash and Matheu, he locked eyes with Oliver one last time before turning and following the grimy group of thieves down the hall to meet their leader and discuss their death wish for Tameer.

For someone who was quite possibly walking to his death, Tameer felt oddly calm. Confident even. He attributed some of that, at least, to the strong-willed, devilishly handsome man at his side. Oliver's hand was resting on the blade at his waist, while the other was at the small of Tameer's back, ready to reel him in if the need arose. Oliver had been very forceful the night before in his demands to accompany Tameer throughout this excursion. He wouldn't be denied.

While Tam felt some guilt about putting the man in harm's way, especially after he just got his brother back, Tameer couldn't help the relief he felt at Oliver's company. The man knew how to fight, for one, but there was something about him that made Tameer stand a little taller.

Not to mention, this was Tameer's former empire. He reigned over this guild for years before being unceremoniously ousted. The Guild was clearly being run into the ground now, but Tameer knew the layout—and the majority of the people—like he knew his own cock. He could handle this shit.

The woman leading them was named Rhea, if Tam remembered correctly, but he was fairly certain she preferred to be called Roach, although he couldn't fathom why. She halted before a rusted iron door, the hinges of which looked ready to give way at the strongest breeze. "Wait here," she commanded gruffly.

Leaving Tam and Oliver with two of the more unwashed, younger-looking henchmen, Roach shouldered the door open and disappeared from sight.

Standing awkwardly in the dimly lit hallway, Tameer tried not to let his nerves get the best of him. This was his plan after all. He couldn't let his fears about what might go wrong get in the way of things now. It was far too late for that anyway.

Oliver's hand on his lower back flexed, griping his kurta and pulling him closer. When Tameer's back pressed against the warmth of the man's solid chest, Oliver whispered directly into Tam's ear. "I've got you. Nothing's going to happen. Just breathe." Oliver's hand released its hold, stroking the length of his spine once, twice, a third time before Roach reemerged.

"Boss is ready." With a grunt, she shoved the door farther open, allowing them entry into the surprisingly well-lit space.

Candles were strewn about the room, in sconces on the walls, hanging from dangerously low chandeliers in the splintered ceiling, and even sat atop piles of strategically placed bricks. At least, Tameer hoped they were strategic. There had to be some level of logic to the madness consuming the space.

"Welcome to our humble home," boomed a voice Tameer knew far too well. Sigrun. Of course it was fucking Sigrun. He was the last of the old world thieves to really thrive under the Guild's abusive tactics. Tameer should have expected he'd be the one to take over and fill the void once he'd left. Fuck everything.

"It's a honor and a privilege, Sig," Tameer said, dropping the nickname knowing how much Sigrun hated it. It was always fun to piss that blood thirsty brute off. Today was no different. The instant rush of blood to the man's face was enough to make Tameer giggle with wicked satisfaction. Internally, of course. On the outside, Tam kept his façade, of cool indifference firmly in place. "Love what you've done with the place. Going for that grunge look, eh? Suits you. I know how deeply you dislike bathing. By the smell of things, it seems you've outlawed them entirely."

"Tam." There was a note of caution in Oliver's voice, but Tameer ignored it.

This was the man who'd been trying to have him killed for years. *Years*. Tameer's sense of self preservation had gone out the window the second he'd laid eyes on the filthy, dimwitted, short-sighted, abusive son of a bitch. Metaphorically, of course. There were no windows in this part of the warehouse. Just gaping holes in the roof.

And the hint of a shadow that looked remarkably like his best friend. Gods, Leah was a magical creature. Tameer was ever grateful to have her on his side.

Seeming to have finally gotten ahold of his tongue, Sigrun growled. "Ye ruttin' bastard. Ye have the balls te come inte my home an' insult me? I should kill ye right now!" He bellowed like a laboring water buffalo. It was beyond mockable. Tameer just shook his head, chuckling to himself.

"If you could have, you would have a long time ago. Let's face it, Sig. You can't kill me. You've been trying years and you just don't have the skill for it." Tameer paused, eyeing Sigrun and openly finding him lacking. "Well, I supposed *you* haven't been trying. You don't have the skill to come for me yourself. You keep sending people. How's that working out for you? Any of them come back with good news yet? Hells, have any of them come back alive?"

Growling, Sigrun pushed up from his makeshift throne—the mangled seat of an old carriage, by all appearances—and drew his sword as he stumbled toward Tameer.

"Oh dear," Tam said with mock concern. "You seem to be a bit unsteady on your feet there, Sig. You feeling okay? I can bring Leah to take a look at you. You know, she's gotten pretty good at the healing thing. Took care of Matheu for our dear friend Oliver here."

Sigrun halted in his bumbling steps. Roach looked between Oliver and Sigrun, thoroughly confused. The grimy men who'd served as the rest of their welcoming party glanced around as well. Interesting.

"Sorry, did I spoil a secret, Sig?" Tameer looked pointedly at the Guild's leader now, narrowing his eyes as he studied the drunken man. Rage flamed anew behind his eyes, but he was too intoxicated to formulate a coherent thought, much less a viable excuse before Tameer revealed his secrets. "You see," Tameer said, turning to the gathering crowd of Guild members. "Oliver's brother Matheu has been sick with red lung for a few years now. Some of you likely know that red lung is treatable, curable, with a simple concoction of herbs and fungi. However, Oliver's family isn't from here. They'd never experienced red lung, or even seen the symptoms before. They didn't understand what was happening to him. So when Sig here told them he could provide medicine to keep him alive and comfortable, they were more than willing to pay the price."

Tameer paused, glancing over at Oliver to make sure he was getting the story right. He'd gotten Oliver's permission to tell this tale, to help sway the Guild to their cause if needed, but Tameer still wanted to make sure that he wasn't upsetting the man. It was a hard story to tell. Oliver had expressly stated that he wouldn't be able to tell it himself. Tameer had offered, and Oliver had willingly accepted.

Seeing the look of unbridled rage in Oliver's eyes now, that vengeful hatred directed at Sigrun, shouldn't have been sexy. But fuck. It really was.

"For years, Oliver and his parents pulled jobs for the Guild under duress. Blackmailed into performing tasks they otherwise never would have just to receive a minimal dose of the medicine rather than a full cure. Sigrun,"—Tameer tossed a casual glance over his shoulder to see the man glancing around furtively—"took advantage of their situation. Rather than helping fellow thieves as the Guild ought, he abused them. All for his own sick gain."

Tameer stepped farther into the room, not to Sigrun's "throne" but until he was firmly in the middle of the room and sure all eyes were on him. More eyes than he'd expected. Apparently, his words had carried and more Guild members had crept into the room while he was speaking. "You might not remember me; it's been a few years since I ran the Guild. My name is Tameer." At the mention of his name, whispers filled the room. Tameer couldn't make out their words, but he didn't think they were all negative. At least, he hoped they weren't. Glancing around the room, Tameer's gaze settled on Oliver. His fist still tightly clenched around his dagger, his attention was now split between Sigrun and Tameer. Tameer gave him a subtle wink, letting him know everything was going according to plan. Well, as according to plan as it could, considering the plan was to get inside and talk.

A small flurry of dust floated down directly in front of Tameer. He didn't have to look up to know Leah had settled herself in the rafters above him. She'd have her weapons ready, in the event that things took a turn. Crossbow. Daggers. Slightly explosive potions. She'd make sure they made it out alive. Ash and Matheu had likely already cleared an exit for them, just in case, and were waiting beyond the door.

Smiling widely at Oliver, Tameer's confidence grew. He could do this. Hells, this was *his* guild. These were *his* people. Sigrun had stolen it all from him and to what end? To fatten himself up while the rest of them toiled away, struggling to fill their bellies, if looks were any indication.

Raising his hands wide, Tameer spoke loudly for all to hear. "You may not know me, but if you ask around, I'm sure you'll hear all sorts of fanciful tales of my tenure as Guild leader. Some true, some wildly exaggerated. All fabulous." He gave them a rakish grin at that, drawing a few quiet laughs from the shadows. Tameer hadn't come here to win back his Guild, but if the gods favored him, that might just be how things played out.

"Ye don' belong 'ere!" Sigrun lunged at Tameer, sword raised above his head, swinging wildly. Tameer jumped back, drawing his own blade and easily blocking the sloppy attack.

"Truly, Sigrun, I think you've proven you aren't meant for this role." Tameer sidestepped another feral attack, smirking while waving off Oliver's attempts to jump in and assist. It might be cocky, but Tameer knew he could handle one drunken, half-ass sword fight.

"Thish," Sigrun grunted, swinging his blade once more. "ish my guild." He slashed unexpectedly to the left, nicking Tameer's sleeve and drawing blood.

The mood changed in an instant. The fun was over. Tameer no longer cared for talking. He wasn't going to reason with Sigrun. He wouldn't have even considered trying, had he known it was Sig running the Guild. Glancing down at the blood that now stained his second favorite pale blue kurta, a sudden wave of unfiltered rage washed over Tameer.

This man, this *abuser*, had taken one of the few things that Tameer had truly cared about. He'd tried to have him killed *several* times. Tameer was done fucking around.

Shifting his stance, Tameer locked his gaze on his target, the stumbling drunk with a look of overconfidence on his dirt smeared face. "I really liked this kurta, you shit." With that, Tameer slashed. His sword came down hard, the sound of metal on metal reverberating throughout the suddenly silent expanse as Sigrun managed to get his blade up in time to block the blow. Tameer didn't back down. Quickly striking again and again. By some miracle, Sigrun managed to block the next two hits, but the third swing of Tameer's blade met flesh. The feel of his sharp metal slicing into soft meat was glorious. Second only to the cry of agony that escaped Sigrun's lips as he fell to the ground. Tameer wrenched his weapon back, attacking again, and again. Blood splattered his clothes, his hands, his face. The warmth of the spray barely registered.

He was panting when Tameer felt strong hands wrap around his waist from behind, lifting him off the ground and carrying him away from his victim. Someone pried the blade from his hands, then took his face in theirs. Gentle, kind, cognac brown eyes stared back at him, thumbs stroking his cheeks. Oliver. His lips were moving, but Tameer's mind didn't register what they were saying.

Oliver pulled him in, wrapping him in his arms and resting his chin on Tameer's head. Curling into him, Tameer unleashed emotions he hadn't realized he'd been holding back. He gripped Oliver's tunic, clenching his fists in the fabric as tears flowed freely down his face.

13

OLIVER HAD KNOWN GOING into the Guild's base was a dangerous plan. He'd been worried about Tameer's safety the whole time. He hadn't once considered that Tameer might unleash his own blood-thirsty rage monster and massacre the leader in front of the entire Guild.

Oliver had been forced to pry the sword from Tameer's fingers, dropping it and pulling the man into his embrace to break the hold the blood-rage had on him. It was unnerving. If it weren't for Leah, Ash, and Matty closing ranks on them, armed and facing the surrounding crowds, Oliver wasn't sure they would have survived. The Guild was stunned, sure, but they were defensive. They might not have all liked Sigrun, but their leader had just been murdered right before their eyes. It wasn't something they could let stand.

There was a heavy silence in the room as the gravity of the situation became clear. Sigrun, the leader of the Thieves' Guild, was dead. The Guild members looked furtively around at one another, seemingly trying to determine who was going to fill the void while sizing up the competition at the same time. The woman who'd brought them to Sigrun drew a short, twisted blade from her boot, moving toward them with her eyes fixed on Tam.

Leah immediately got in the woman's way. "What's the plan, darlin'? You think you can beat me, and him, and him, and *him*? Then kill Tam and take the Guild for yourself? Madame Luck is not on your side tonight. Sorry, dear." Her own blade glinted in the candlelight, shining with the threat of violence and certain death.

Tameer's tears had calmed as he lifted his head from Oliver's chest and eyed the woman. She still hadn't taken her eyes off him, despite Leah's open threats. Taking one more step, she got down on her knees and raised her weapon, offering him the hilt as she held it by the blade.

What the hells was going on?

Tameer loosened his hold on Oliver, patting his chest and stepping away, toward the woman now offering her neck? What the actual fuck was going on? Leah pulled Ash aside, giving Tameer space to approach the woman and accept her proffered blade. He studied it, testing the weight, pricking the tip of his thumb with it before looking down at the kneeling woman.

His face still glistened with the last of his tears, but Tameer's ferocity was unmatched. Staring out at the gathered Guild members, he looked like a viking king of old. Demanding retribution from those who betrayed him. At least, that's how it appeared to Oliver. Tameer hadn't struck him as the type to seek blood payment, but he also hadn't seemed like the type to cut a man to pieces. Clearly, Oliver didn't know the man as well as he thought.

"How many of you were here when I ran the Guild?" Tameer asked the room.

A handful of individuals stepped forward, none looking directly at Tameer, all seemingly ashamed.

"Come on, now. I recognize more faces than that. There's no need to hide. I'm just curious to see who all is still here." Tameer's voice was confident, despite the rasp in his throat.

Several more came forward. By the looks of things, only about a dozen members were new to Tameer. They were all new to Oliver, but he'd rarely bothered stepping foot in the Guild's headquarters. He'd wanted as little to do with them as possible.

Tameer studied the woman kneeling before him once more. Oliver watched as she tilted her head farther back, giving him easier access to her jugular. Gods, was she offering herself as a sacrifice? What the fuck was this place? Oliver moved to step in, but Leah put a hand on his shoulder. A single shake of her head stayed his movement. Whatever was going on, he needed to let Tameer handle it. He'd promised not to interfere unless Tameer was in danger. He had to respect that.

Tameer had always hated this tradition. It was barbaric and fucking idiotic. They weren't werewolves. Hells, they weren't animals of any kind. Why the hells would the Guild adopt such disgusting forms of punishment for disobedience? It baffled the mind.

Roach waited with more patience than Tameer had ever seen the woman possess. He let the seconds drag out longer than he probably ought to have, just to see if she'd move. Truly, she'd matured since he'd been gone.

But he was being cruel, and he was rarely cruel.

Dropping to his knees, he set the blade on the ground between them, resting his hands on either side of her proffered neck.

"There will be no letting today. Nor ever again, so long as I'm your leader." He lifted her face until her eyes met his. "Assuming you'll have me?"

Confusion flickered in Roach's eyes, chased quickly away by realization that her blood wouldn't be spilled, her life spared. Tears lined her lashes, although she'd never let anyone see them. The Guild—especially under leaders like Sigrun—abhorred emotional outburst. Tears were a sign of weakness. Which was one of the reasons why Tameer took pride in openly showing all of his emotions. Fuck the old ways. Emotions of all kind were welcome in his Guild. Even the embarrassing ones. Hells, *especially* the embarrassing ones.

Roach nodding in his hands, quickly blinking her tears away. Tameer rose, helping her to her feet and handing her blade back.

"I understand that the Guild is currently looking for a new leader." He looked pointedly to the bloody remains of Sigrun. Tameer's lips involuntarily curled into a sneer. Refocusing on the living members, he continued. "If you're interested, I'd like to volunteer for the position."

To his surprise and delight, the room filled with cheers of excitement and welcome.

Tameer was finally home.

14

THE NEXT FEW DAYS passed in a blur of packing, cleaning, moving, and purging.

Purging of garbage both physical and human.

Oliver was shocked by the drastic changes the man had made in less than a week, including removing all members who were loyal to Sigrun and his vile, abusive "training methods." Tameer hadn't been playing around when he'd said he wanted to clean up the Guild. With Leah's help, many of the older, most violent members of the old generation were removed from their positions after just one night of overindulgent drinking. It was very effective, if a bit dark and brutal.

Oliver probably should have been upset by the behavior, but after spending time with the children—some barely old enough to wipe their own ass—and hearing the horror stories of how they'd been treated, Oliver had no sympathy for the loss of those members. Leah's poisons had been too good for them.

The Guild's warehouse had a convenient furnace in the basement, in which Matty, Ash, and Oliver spent days disposing of the corpses while providing heat for the entire Guild. It was a very "full circle" moment, honestly. Their deaths were able to benefit the Guild one last time.

Over breakfast the next week, Tameer laid out his plans.

"Leah and I have gone through the books. Which is to say, we dug through every disgusting nook and cranny in this shit hole and collected all the coin we could find. It's not much, but it should be enough to patch the roof and the majority of the holes in the walls. We'll need to start working the Guild as a group. Finding high value targets and bringing in revenue so that we can rebuild this place." There was a brightness in Tameer's eyes that Oliver had never seen before. Eagerness and excitement. This was a man who knew what he wanted. It was sexy as hells, but Oliver couldn't help feeling a bit left out in the cold. He had no interest in helping the Guild raise funding. He didn't want to steal for the sake of stealing.

Oliver had his own goal. Now that his brother was healthy and Tameer was safe, he needed to find a way to free his parents from that merchant's dungeon. They weren't officially under arrest. There would be no trial. The royal courts would likely not be involved at all, not that thieves were granted fair trials in the first place. Although, Oliver had to admit, they *were* guilty. They'd been caught attempting to rob some foreign rug merchant of his prized family jewels. Literal jewels. They'd verified that information. Twice.

Oliver was glad Tameer had found his purpose and was safe and happy, but he had his own business to attend to. He needed to grab Matty and get going. They couldn't stick around here any longer.

"I wish you the best of luck. I have no doubt you'll get it all back up and running in no time." Oliver took a bite of his oatmeal, cold and a bit gritty, but he was never one to complain about a free meal he hadn't had to cook.

Tameer cocked an eyebrow. "Why does that sound like the start of a shitty goodbye?"

Leah and Ash shared a look, then promptly took their bowls and left the room, abandoning Oliver to address the situation he'd been hoping to avoid. It might have been spineless, but he'd secretly been hoping to slip out while Tameer was busy. Leave a note and fuck off without having to actually say anything.

Seeing the confusion in Tameer's face now, Oliver knew he was a bastard. He was a fucking weak coward who would rather run away than hurt this man's feelings.

"It's just," he began, dipping his spoon in the cold oatmeal, praying to whatever god might be listening that they might strike him dead now. Then he wouldn't have to come up with an explanation or try to find the words he didn't want to have to say. "I, well, Matty and I. We were never really part of the Guild by choice, you know? My parents. Our parents. We were all forced into this." He gestured vaguely around them. "We didn't choose this life. We had our own system before. It worked well for us. The Guild stole that from us. And now my parents, well, fuck. I mean, they're still locked away in some dungeon." Oliver ground his teeth. He wasn't explaining anything well. This was what Matty called word vomit. When Oliver couldn't form coherent thoughts and just spilled everything all at once. It was embarrassing and unhelpful, but he couldn't seem to make it stop. "I can't stay here," he blurted out. "*We* can't stay here. We have to get them back. The Guild is important to you, and I completely understand that. This place was your family for years. But this is *my* family and they need me."

Tameer sat back in his chair, crossing his arms over his chest as he watched Oliver. Wiping a hand over his face, Oliver released a frustrated groan. Why was he so fucking bad at this?

Burying his face in his hands, he closed his eyes and sighed.

He heard the sound of Tameer's chair being pushed back, and footsteps as the man crossed the room. He was leaving. Of course he was. Oliver had just diminished everything that was important to him. Why the hells would he stay? Not to mention, Oliver had made it clear *he* was leaving. There was no reason for Tameer to stick around now if Oliver was already halfway out the door.

Gentle, calloused hands slipped under the collar of Oliver's tunic. Bolting upright, Oliver nearly headbutt Tameer as the man leaned in.

"I know your family is important to you." Tameer's voice was as smooth as velvet. His hands kneaded the tight knots at the base of Oliver's neck. "Why the hells do you think Leah and I spent the last two nights mapping out the layout of the rug merchant's home? Finding all the best ingress and egress points. Selecting the best crew for the job." His hands worked magic as his words melted away the last of Oliver's anxiety. "Your family might not have chosen to be a part of the Guild, but they are a part of it now, nonetheless. We never leave people behind. We're going to get them back. Tonight."

As Oliver and Matty checked their weapons in the shoddy room they'd chosen for their own, Oliver's mind was spinning. Tameer had taken the time to plan a rescue for his parents. While in the midst of a very messy take over and reconstruction for the Guild, he'd made Oliver's family a priority. Oliver was so used to taking care of everyone else, he couldn't wrap his mind around the idea that someone else might step in and carry some of the burden for him.

"Did he tell you the plan, then? Or are we just blindly following Guild orders again?" Matty seemed more than a little annoyed, which Oliver couldn't understand.

"What's your deal? Tameer is *helping* us free our parents after the Guild left them to rot in that damned dungeon. This is a good thing, you twit."

"We shouldn't even be here anymore, Oli." Matty tossed a nervous look at the open doorway. He'd been anxious since they'd crossed the threshold of the Guild's headquarters days ago. With good reason, Oliver knew, but with Tameer running the Guild, things were already running different and considerably more smoothly.

"You think Mom and Pop will care who we're working with if it means they're free? We aren't indebted to the Guild anymore, Matty. Tam is helping us because he can. Because he knows it's the right thing to do." It annoyed Oliver to no end that he had to justify their working relationship with Tameer. Matty *knew* Tameer. They'd spent enough time with the man to know his motives and understand his mind.

Matty gnawed on his lower lip, glancing toward the doorway once more. "He's not the one I'm worried about," he whispered.

"What the hells is going on?" Oliver stepped closer to his brother, placing a firm hand on his shoulder. "What's got you so rattled?"

Matty's eyes darted around the room, anxiety coming off him in waves. His gaze finally settled on Oliver as he spoke, voice barely audible over the hum of activity in the warehouse. "I overheard something last night. Voices planning a coup. They aren't happy that Tameer's back. They want him gone. For good."

For fuck's sake. Can't things ever go right?

"So you and Oliver will take the east side. Roach will take Matheu on the west. Ash and I will take the south." Leah was standing over the hand-drawn map of the rug merchant's home, going over the plan with Tameer one last time. Tameer, however, was barely listening. The look of shock on Oliver's face still burned into his mind.

Had Oliver truly believed that Tameer would forget about him? About his parents? After everything the Guild had put them through, freeing them was the least he could do. He fully intended to do much more, but getting them out of the dungeon was the first step.

Leah snapped impatiently in his face. "Are you even listening?"

Tameer smirked, shaking his head. "Sadly, no. I've been tuning you out for the last half hour. I know the plan, love. I don't need to be treated like a child on my first mission. We've done this countless times before."

Hand on hip, Leah quirked an eyebrow. "Aye, we've done this before, but it's been quite some time since you were out in the field. And you went a little nuts the other night with Sigrun. I don't need a berserker on this mission, Tam. I get enough of that with Ash. I need you focused. Light on your feet and quick with the lock picks. Can you do that? If not, I'll find someone else. You can stay here. It's not a big deal and it's certainly not shameful if you need to stay out of this one." Her words were harsh, but there was no bite to them. Leah was mission oriented. It was one of the things he loved about her—although that didn't take the sting out.

"I'm fine." Tameer tried to keep the edge from his voice. He was *mostly* fine. Sigrun had been a vile, abusive man and Tam had no regrets about what he'd done. Still, he hadn't actually intended to kill them man. He only barely remembered doing it, honestly.

Leah studied him for a moment, then moved around the small table and took his hands in hers. "Tam, what's going on?"

She'd dropped the serious, assassin-planning-a-job voice and was giving him her full attention. Her purple eyes sparkled with a hint of worry.

How the hells was he supposed to ignore that?

"It's nothing," he started, but she squeezed his hands, not letting him get away with that. Sighing, he pulled her into a hug, resting his chin on her head. "What if he leaves?" He spoke into her rose gold hair, afraid to look her in the eyes and let her see the vulnerability in his.

Leah wrapped her arms around his waist, hugging him tightly. "Then he's a fucking idiot," she said, her cheek pressed to his chest.

A small chuckle escaped his lips.

"Is that what all this is about? Truly?" She didn't pull away as she spoke, but Tameer could hear the incredulity in her voice. He pictured the way her eyebrow was raised, a look of confusion and disbelief on her face.

"It's stupid, I know. But he's the first person I've cared about." She huffed indignantly and started to pull back, but Tameer tightened his hold on her and corrected his words. "The first person I've cared about *like this*. Romantically. I honestly didn't think I'd ever feel like this about anyone. Once we get his parents back, he's got no reason to stick around."

"Gods, you are brilliant, but you are such an idiot some-times." Leah laughed into his kurta, shaking her head ever-so-slightly.

"Rude." Tameer pulled back a bit to look her in the eye. "Why would you say that?"

A bemused smile tugged at Leah's lips as she studied him for a beat too long.

"What is it?" he prodded.

"You really don't see it, do you?"

"See what? Stop being so cryptic. Subtlety doesn't suit you."

Leah swatted his arm, then pulled him back in for a quick hug. "That man is head over heels for you, you blind idiot." Releasing him, she flounced across the room and retrieved a decanter of amber liquid and two highball glasses.

Tameer gaped at her. How could she be so glib? "Darling, I think you might be the blind one. It's just sex. He doesn't care about me. Not like that."

Leah poured two glasses before handing one to him. "If you truly believe that, you haven't been paying any attention. You've gone and gotten yourself so... how did you put it be-fore? *Entangled* in love that you can't even see that the man feels the same fucking way. Was I that dense too? Fuck. Love makes people insufferable."

Tameer swallowed his drink in one. As the liquor burned its way down his throat, he let his mind wander through the interactions he'd had with Oliver of late. Hot and sexy, without a doubt, but had there been more to it on Oliver's end?

I go where you go.

Gods. What if Leah was right? Was he an idiot?

<h1 style="text-align:center">15</h1>

OLIVER DEBATED HOW AND when to inform Tameer about the supposed threat on his life. It wasn't that he didn't believe Matty's intel, but his brother had precious little by way of details, so the information was next to useless. Someone—or someone*s*—in the Guild wanted to kill Tam and usurp his newly reacquired power. That wasn't exactly headline news, considering the place was filled with thieves and murderers.

Oliver was pacing the chambers outside Tameer's "office" when he nearly walked straight into Ash.

"Watch it," the mountain grumbled, catching Oliver by the shoulders and righting him before he fell on his ass.

"Shit. Sorry. I was distracted." Running a hand through his hair, Oliver turned to resume his pacing, but Ash caught his arm, halting his progress.

There was a look in Ash's eyes that Oliver couldn't place. It almost looked like concern, but that would be ridiculous, wouldn't it? Still, Ash kept his grip firm, but not rough, as he led Oliver down the hall and into an empty room, shouldering the door closed. "Talk," he commanded, releasing his hold on Oliver's arm and leaning against the door.

Oliver got the impression that while Ash was currently blocking the exit, he wasn't trapped. The man was acting more as a barricade to stop unwelcome intruders than as a captor.

"I don't know—"

"No." Ash cut him off. "Something is going on. Tell me now or I'll go find out from that little brother of yours. He seems amenable to friendly chats."

Oliver knew it was an empty threat, but the urge to keep his brother from this man was overwhelming nonetheless. "Someone is plotting to kill Tam."

Ash huffed. "No shit. That's not new." Crossing his arms across the massive expanse of his chest, Ash seemed thoroughly unbothered.

"Someone is plotting to kill Tam *soon*," Oliver continued. "Matheu overheard some members talking about it last night. They don't like how he came in and took over. They're planning a coup. The only problem is that Matty didn't see who was talking and he didn't recognize any voices. He couldn't even tell how many voices there were."

"So what you're saying is we have almost no information on a potentially viable and immediate threat to Tameer's life?" Ash pushed off the wall, dropping his arms and clenching his fists.

Oliver nodded.

"Shit. Leah's not gonna like that." Ash blew out an annoyed sigh. Stepping aside, he pried the door back open and gestured for Oliver to follow him. They strode down the hall again, Ash leading with purpose, and barged into Tameer's office.

Tameer and Leah were lounging on the rotten couch, drinking from highball glasses and laughing deliriously. Leah's cheeks were flushed and Oliver was sure Tam's would have been too, if not for his coppery complexion that largely hide his intoxication.

"Fuck everything," Ash muttered. He shoved the door closed behind them, then jammed a chair against it so the door wouldn't open without a great deal of force.

"What's wrong, love?" Leah cooed, pulling a pink curl from her hair and wrapping it playfully around her finger. "Did you want to join us? I'm sure Tam wouldn't mind sharing." She tossed him a saucy wink to which Tameer responded with a dramatic gag.

"Are you *drunk*?" Oliver didn't hide his shock. They had a mission in a few hours. A mission to save his parents and the two planning the damn thing were drunk off their asses in the middle of the gods damned day.

Tameer rose unsteadily, grabbing the arm of the couch and stumbling toward Oliver. "I most certainly am... not." His eyes shimmered in the candlelight, but it was clear they were unfocused.

"I can't fucking believe this." Ash raked a hand through his hair, glaring at his boots. "This is really shit timing, Leah. We need to talk. Serious talk."

Leah perked up a bit at his tone. Sobering just enough to understand the need for clear-headedness. "What is it? What changed?"

Ash said nothing as he crossed the room to the fireplace. He grabbed a chair along the way and began smashing it to pieces. Leah didn't even attempt to hide her amusement at watching his show of brute strength. Once he'd gotten the wood placed, he searched for kindling or some way to start a fire. Finding nothing, he began muttering curses to himself. Oliver couldn't understand them, but he knew the sentiment well enough, he didn't need to hear the exact words.

"I've got it, love." Leah stumbled to the fireplace, reaching into one of the many pouches attached to her belt. Ash caught her right before she went headlong into the brick herself. She beamed up at him, raising a hand and tossing a pinch of some-thing into the fireplace. A loud pop was quickly followed by the crackling of flames. Whatever that powder was, it worked well as a fire-starter.

"Go," Ash commanded as he set Leah back down on her feet. "Sit." He turned her toward a chair and gave her a gentle push.

"Oooh, I do love when he gets bossy," she said with a wink to Oliver.

Tameer was half-standing, half-leaning against the couch staring unseeingly into the flames while Ash set a kettle on the hook over the fire. He was making coffee. Good man. He in-tended the sober them up. He'd clearly been around these two long enough to know how to handle them at their drunkest.

A sudden pang of jealousy shot through Oliver at the thought. He'd never get the chance to learn all of Tameer's quirks. He'd never learn how best to handle his moods or cater to his needs.

Once they retrieved his parents, Oliver would be gone. He would leave with his family and likely never see Tameer again.

Gods, why did that thought hurt so much?

The coffee was disgusting, but it did the trick. Tameer hadn't intended to drink the entire bottle of whisky with Leah, but once they got started, they didn't stop. It had been so long since they'd hung out, just the two of them. It felt like the old days, if only for a little while.

Then Oliver and Ash had come crashing in, ruining all their fun and sobering the situation up in the most depressing way.

The look on Oliver's face alone had a sobering effect. He'd been so hurt to find Tameer drunk with Leah instead of skillfully planning a flawless rescue of his parents so he could finally be free to leave.

Well, Tam assumed that was the reason. The man wanted his parents out of a dungeon. That wasn't unreasonable. Tam felt like a selfish asshole for even thinking such harsh thoughts, but the longer Chantrelle and Enoki were imprisoned, the longer Oliver would stick around.

Gods, he was the worst.

Unfortunately, now that the coffee had worked its villainous magic, Tameer was sober enough to understand the severity of the problem Oliver brought to them.

An unnamed assailant or assailants wanted to kill him and take the Guild.

Tameer had expected a coup would happen sooner or later, but he was really hoping to at least get through the first month. Madame Luck wasn't on his side, it would seem. She rarely was, these days.

Tameer swallowed the dregs of his coffee, pursing his lips at the grittiness of it. "What do you propose, King's Guard?" Protection had been Ash's job for years. Tameer would be a fool not to listen to his advice now.

Ash leaned against the back of the couch Leah was lounging on. She'd refused the coffee. Leah was physically incapable of drinking coffee without twelve scoops of sugar, nutmeg, cinnamon, and cream. Black coffee found in the bottom drawer of a random cabinet in the Guild's falling-apart headquarters? As she said, "Fuck off."

"Is there anyone here you trust?" It was a fair question, but not one Tameer liked. Only because the answer was depressing.

"Yes, but the list is very short."

Ash narrowed his eyes. "How short?"

"Three names."

A low whistle escaped Leah's still-drunken lips. "That's not much. More than I expected though. Good for you! Making friends."

"We'll start there, then. Get those three to help us narrow down who might be planning this coup and when they plan to attack." Ash absentmindedly stroked a hand through Leah's rose-gold waves.

Jealousy rocked through Tameer like an earthquake.

Shaking his head, he tried to ignore the feeling.

Oliver stood across the room, arm on the mantle as he glared at the flames.

"I'll give you the names. We can start that shit tomorrow. We have a job tonight that can't wait."

Oliver's head snapped up, instantly finding Tameer's eyes. Confusion and shock lingered on his face.

"Are you sure that's a good idea?" Ash asked. His voice was cautious. It was clear he didn't think a job of any kind was smart with a threat eminent.

Tam nodded, never breaking eye contact with Oliver. "They've waited far too long. We're getting them back tonight. Everything else will wait."

16

M ATTY HAD SPLIT OFF with Roach, having been assigned to create a distraction on the west side of the building, while Leah and Ash were entering through the south to ensure their exit route. Oliver and Tameer crept along in the shadows along the east side of the ostentatious "home," ducking under brightly lit windows and deftly avoiding eye contact.

Oliver knew they needed to discuss whatever it was between them, but he didn't know how. He'd half hoped Tameer would make the decision for him by being an ass or abandoning his parents like the rest of the Guild had been willing to do. Instead, this gods damned man was stalking through the night, risking his own neck to save people he'd never met for *Oliver*. Because they were important to *Oliver*.

Which was an answer in its own right.

But he still couldn't be sure.

For all Oliver knew, Tameer was doing this to set things right with the Guild and it had literally nothing to do with Oliver and how he may or may not feel. Tam had an odd sense of pride and honor about the Guild and how they should conduct business. Leaving members behind clearly violated that code. Perhaps that's all this was.

They reached the servants entrance as the bells tolled three. Prime time for a little breaking and entering, according to Roach. Before the baker would be up to start the day's bread, and after all the drunk guards had finally passed out for the night. The estate would be left with a skeleton crew, which would be drawn to the "small but smoky" explosion Roach would set off on the west side in three... two...

BOOM

The explosion was far from small, shaking Oliver's teeth as he crouched down behind the wall, bracing against the impact.

"What the fuck?" he swore under his breath.

"I said *small*, dammit," Tameer hissed.

They sat frozen in the shadows for a few heartbeats, listening to the shouts of guards as they raced away, heading toward the explosion.

"Now," Tameer whispered, grabbing the handle and pulling the door open as quietly as possible. Not that it would have mattered, the kitchens they entered were completely empty. The echoes of booted footsteps receded down the halls as they crept farther into the building. "The dungeon is in the root cellar. Hang a left up ahead."

Oliver followed Tam's directions, momentarily wondering why the man with the map in his head wasn't leading the way. Then he heard the subtle hiss of Tameer's daggers being unsheathed. Tossing a quick glance over his shoulder, he understood what Tam was doing. Walking backward, Tameer was guarding Oliver and guiding him at the same time. It was arrogant and foolhardy. The sight made Oliver's heart swell.

Focus, he reminded himself. Taking a left as directed, he found a thick wooden door that opened to a dark, dank stone stairway. Drawing his own weapon, Oliver checked to ensure Tameer was still right behind him, then began their descent.

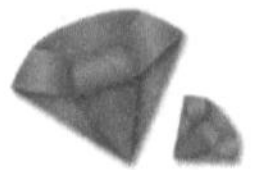

The root cellar seemed to be more of a storage space for moldy flour and rotting boxes of apples, but Tameer didn't spare it much attention. As soon as they were both safely within the confines of the cellar, he pulled the door firmly closed, barricading it shut with a cast iron poker he'd swiped from the kitchen hearth. They wouldn't be exiting that way anyway.

"There should be another door down that way." He motioned for Oliver to head northwest, following the faintest hint of light. It appeared the rug merchant wasn't so cruel as to keep his dungeons pitch black. Pretty damn close, though.

"You blocked the door," Oliver observed. He was surprisingly calm, considering Tameer hadn't actually informed him of this particular portion of the plan.

"Yes, I did. Once the guards figure out the explosion was intentional, they'll come looking for a reason. I gave them a place to look."

Oliver stopped walking, turning to face Tameer. In the near-total darkness, Tam couldn't make out Oliver's expression, but he got the impression it was something along the lines of *What the hells for?*

"We're part two of the distraction," Tameer stated matter-of-factly. Side-stepping around Oliver, he sheathed his daggers and continued on toward the dungeon. It was a good half mile walk and they were on a schedule. They would have to argue—sorry, *talk*—and walk.

Oliver stood dumbfounded for a few moments, then jogged to catch up. "What the fuck are you on about? What second distraction? Distraction for what?"

"The job, obviously." Tameer was being cryptic, but it was fun, and he so rarely got to have this kind of fun anymore. Not to mention, Oliver would be gone soon and he'd never have the chance to tease the man again.

Growling, Oliver grabbed Tameer by the arm, shoving him against the wall and pressing his forearm into Tam's neck. Not hard enough to cause damage, but definitely enough to send Tam's blood rushing in the wrong direction. Well, not *wrong*, but definitely inconvenient for their current situation.

"Tell me what is going on," Oliver demanded. He pressed his body against Tameer's, practically grinding against him. Tam didn't even try to quell the moan that slipped from his lips.

Pressing harder against him, Oliver leaned in, his lips brushing the shell of Tameer's ear as he commanded, "Explain yourself."

Oh, gods. He was good. Pain as a form of torture was one thing, but this? This was a torment that Tameer would happily crack under in seconds.

Tameer felt an unexpected sharp pain as Oliver's teeth sank into the sensitive flesh just below his earlobe. The pain was wiped away just as quickly with a lap of Oli's warm tongue and a soft kiss. "Last chance. Next time, I won't take the sting away." The roughness in Oliver's voice was like a drug. Tameer would have done anything the man said.

"We're rescuing your parents." Gods, was that his voice? So weak and breathy. Tameer barely recognized it.

Grinding against him again, Oliver shifted his arm and bit harder into Tam's neck. There were no kisses this time, though. "What else?" he prompted.

Groaning, Tameer debated answering. If he held out, Oliver would continue this line of torture, which was *highly* enjoyable. But they were on a clock, and as much as Tameer wanted to play this scene out, they really needed to keep moving. Fuck. Being responsible was the fucking worst.

"Leah is currently in the merchant's safe, stealing all his jewels." Tameer said it all on a single exhale, then reached up to slide his fingers through Oliver's hair. Maybe they had a little time. A quickie in the dark dungeon hall would be exhilarating...

Oliver stepped back before Tameer could get a firm grip on him. "Good boy," was all he said as he turned and continued down the hall as though nothing had happened.

Adjusting himself, Oliver fought the urge to turn back and finish what he'd started with Tameer. Gods, he really needed to get his head examined. His cock had nearly taken full control of the situation and thrown their entire plan out the gods damned window.

Taking several deep, calming breaths, Oliver let the overwhelming scent of decay and body odor kill the mood. They arrived at the dungeon. A thick iron gate stood between them and the dungeon proper, as well as a single guard who'd clearly been left behind while the rest went to investigate the explosion.

The guard seemed young, his helmet fitting a tad too large on his head, sliding over his eyes as he repeatedly forced it back up. His ill-fitting tunic was synched tight around his waist by a length of rope. Oliver almost felt bad for the kid. He'd been abandoned at this shit posting while the others raced off to see what all the excitement was about. He wasn't at all prepared for what was about to happen.

A wet cough echoed farther down the dungeon hall.

Oliver's pity for the young guard vanished.

His parents were locked away in this dungeon. Fuck this kid and his shitty comrades. Tameer placed a hand on Oliver's shoulder, the signal that he was ready for entry. Oliver stepped to the side, giving Tameer access to the lock on the gate. Tameer made quick work of picking the ancient lock then he stepped back once more. Oliver had insisted on being the first to enter any space. Tam hadn't liked it, but Oliver had refused to hear any arguments. These were *his* parents, not to mention, they wouldn't trust Tameer on sight. It had to be Oliver.

Plus, Oliver needed to be the first in, as a safety precaution. He couldn't risk something happening to Tameer. Although he didn't give himself a chance to look into that thought too deeply.

The gate swung open with an ominous creak. The young guard turned to face them, but his helm fell. "What happened? What was all the ruckus about?" he asked as he set his weapon down to right the helm once again.

Poor kid never stood a chance. Oliver jumped him, whacking the top of the guard's iron helmet with the pommel of his dagger. A loud ringing echoed throughout the dungeon as the kid fell to the ground unconscious.

"Efficient," Tameer said with a nod of admiration. He pulled some rope from one of the pouches on his belt and bound the young guard's wrists to his ankles. Oliver snatched the ring of keys off a hook on the wall as Tameer grabbed a torch and made his way toward the cells.

There were only six cells in the dungeon. All this time, Oliver had been picturing more of a prison, with dozens of cells and hundreds of prisoners. In fact, his parents were the *only* beings in the cells.

"Mom? Pop?" Oliver reached through the bars, squinting in the darkness to try and make out their shapes in the shadows.

Tameer held the light aloft, but kept his distance as best he could. He was giving Oliver the space he needed to reconnect with his parents.

"Oli? Is that you, baby?" His mom's voice cracked. Stepping into the light, she looked considerably thinner than she had when he'd last seen her.

"What the hells are you doing here, son?" Fuck. If his mother looked thin, his father was gaunt. Oliver knew without question that his father had been giving his mother more food than he'd been eating himself. That damned man loved her more than himself and he would always put her needs before his own.

"We're here to get you out." Oliver nodded to Tameer over his shoulder then set about trying keys to open the gate.

"Wait..." Mom began. "Aren't you..."

"No, he's supposed to be dead, ain't he?" Pop chimed in, eyeing Tameer with obvious admiration and suspicion.

Tameer smiled warmly at them. "Aye, I'm him. And yes, I'm supposed to be dead a few times over. That's actually how I met your lovely boys."

The door clicked open, saving Oliver from having to tell that story. For now. "We need to go. Can you both walk?"

Pop raised an incredulous eyebrow at him as if to say, *Who the hells do you think you're talking to?* Then he took Mom's hand and they strolled out of the cell as though they were going for a peaceful morning picnic.

17

CHANTRELLE AND ENOKI. GODS, they were *famous*. And they knew who *he* was? Tameer was walking on fucking clouds as he led them out through the tunnels Roach had uncovered. The tunnels were apparently part of an old smuggling network from the time of the Red King. The Red King's disdain for all things fun—drugs, alcohol, etc.—led to a plethora of clever schemes and underground passageways that enabled the revelries to continue. When the Red King was overthrown some sixty years ago, the revelries were allowed to come out of the shadows and the majority of the smuggling passages were forgotten. Thank the gods for Roach and her incredibly thorough research.

Tameer stayed a few steps ahead of Oliver and his parents, wanting to give them space, and pointedly avoided listening in on anything that they might be saying to each other. He could hear their voices, but made a conscious effort to ignore their words so he wouldn't violate this moment. While Tam didn't know exactly how long Chantrelle and Enoki had been locked away, he knew it had been far too long and it had taken a heavy toll on Oliver.

A hint of dawn began to brighten the end of the tunnel. Tameer doused the torch in one of the many muddy puddles and pushed back the overgrown branches to reveal a small stream, two row boats, and the rest of their crew.

Matheu leapt up at the sight of his parents, racing over to them and wrapping his mother in a hug so tight Tameer almost worried for the woman's ability to breathe. Enoki clapped his hand on his son's back and was quickly pulled into a hug as well. Soon, all four of them were wrapped in a tear-filled embrace and Tameer slipped away to join the rest of their crew by the boats to avoid feeling like an interloper.

"Did you get it all?" he asked Leah.

Grinning widely, she pulled out a canvas bag from one of the boats and opened it to show off a stunning collection of sparkling gemstones. Sapphires, diamonds, citrines, emeralds, rubies, and that was just what he could see in the dim morning light. Tameer let out a low whistle as he admired their new collection. "This will set us up nicely."

"I thought so, too. Maybe have a few set into jewelry and even sell them back to that arrogant fool." Leah's smirk was borderline maniacal at the prospect. Tameer *loved* the idea.

"I'll need to find a new jeweler. My connections have likely all dried up. I've been out for too long." Tameer started making a mental list of all the people he used to know and who might still be in the game now.

"What kind of jewelry are you looking to have made? I've got some skill in the craft." Chantrelle's voice startled Tameer. He hadn't realized the woman had joined them. Gods, she was quite stealthy. Either that or he'd really let his guard down. He'd need to work on that now that he was back in the Guild.

Leah fished two rubies the size of her pinky nail out of the sack and handed them to Chantrelle. "Maybe some earrings? Set in gold or silver if you can?"

Chantrelle turned the stones over in her hands, admiring the cut and shape of them. "Aye, I can do it. It's been a minute since I've done any smithing, but it's like picking a lock. The muscle memory is there. Just gotta get some supplies." She turned to look at Tameer. "If it's all right with you, I mean. I hear it's your Guild now, so it's your call."

Schooling his face so as to not give away the feel of shock that rocked him at the idea of *Chantrelle* deferring to him, Tameer smiled graciously. "I would be honored to have you with us for as long as you'd like."

Oliver held his tongue the entire ride back to the Guild's warehouse. He poured his nervous energy into rowing the boat and formulating his argument in his mind. He needed to have this out. He needed things settled so he could move on.

They moored the boats at a small pier outside the warehouse, then he and Matty led their parents to the room they'd adopted as their own. Mom and Pop ate a hearty meal of far too many baked goods—it seemed Leah could bake anything anywhere—and a deer felled by Ash, then went to bed. Although, not before Mom gave Roach a list of supplies she'd need to begin gold and silver smithing.

Oliver vaguely recalled a time when his mother was a smith. It had been when he and Matty were still learning the grift. They'd settled in a large city where they could go mostly unnoticed, but Mom plied her trade as an honest jewelry smith while Pop taught the boys the family business. When she'd said it had "been a minute," Oliver had wanted to correct her. It had been more like fifteen years. But if she was confident in her skills, who was he to argue?

"What the hells, man? You're going to wear a hole right through the floor if you keep pacing like that." Matty tossed a stale roll at Oliver, knocking him out of his thoughts and ensuring he had Oliver's full attention. "What's wrong with you? They're home! I'm healthy. Everything is good. Why are you acting like the world is ending?"

Because, for me, it still is, he wanted to say. His parents never stayed in one place for too long. Their family was always on the move. Nomadic, his father had called them. It was safer that way. They'd stay long enough to make the jewelry as Mom had promised—likely she felt like she owed Tameer for the rescue, despite it being the Guild's fault that they'd been imprisoned in the first place—and then they'd be gone again. Oliver just got them back. He sure as hells wasn't going to let them go without him. Which meant he would be leaving Tameer.

But that was fine, right? He barely knew Tam. Hells, they'd only just met a few weeks ago. It wasn't like he was in love with the man or anything. Right?

Right...?

"I'm fine. Just ready to get on with it." Oliver picked up the roll his brother had thrown at him, tossed it into the hearth, and turned to leave. "I'm going for a walk. I need some air."

Tameer sat on the dock, dangling his bare feet in the cool water and staring up at the night sky. Oliver's family was whole. He'd sent Roach and Hellbore—one of the few other members Tam truly trusted—into Ravendale to sell off a couple of the smaller gemstones they'd pilfered and buy the materials Chantrelle said she'd need for smithing. Things were moving in the right direction. Finally. Still, Tameer felt like he was waiting for the other shoe to drop. The end was near, as they say, and he knew it was only a matter of time before something else went wrong.

And he feared he knew exactly what it was.

"Oh, shit. I didn't think anyone would be out here." Oliver's voice sounded almost as startled as Tameer felt. "I'll go. Didn't mean to interrupt whatever you're doing."

He quickly turned on his heels to leave, but Tameer spoke up. "You don't have to go." Oliver froze, swaying as though weighing his options. "I'm not doing anything. Just thinking. You're welcome to join me," Tam offered. He knew it was a dangerous choice. The more time he spent with Oliver, the more it was going to hurt when Oliver finally left. And he would leave. Tam wasn't an idiot. Oliver would go with his family.

People always leave. Irena and Leah were the only exceptions, and realistically, hadn't they left too? Leah had left Ravendale to retire from assassinating and live a quieter life in Vexia. Sure, life hadn't stayed quiet and Tameer had ended up joining her, but she'd *left*. And Irena had left them to ultimately live in the gods damned castle. He was so happy for her, of course, but she was yet another person who'd left.

Oliver would be no different, but Tameer couldn't help himself. He was a glutton for pain, apparently.

"If you're sure you don't mind," Oliver finally replied, turning and joining him on the dock. He crossed his legs, resting his elbows on his knees and stared out into the woods across the water.

The silence that stretched between them wasn't quite peaceful, but it wasn't unpleasant either. It was weighty, as they both clearly had things that needed to be said, but neither were interested in breaking the moment.

They sat in companionable quiet, listening to the sounds of the night as the stars danced across the sky. The moon was at her zenith when Tameer finally broke the silence between them.

"I've always abhorred the concept of love. I thought it solely for the weak and made one vulnerable." Tam didn't look at him as he spoke, choosing to continue staring unseeingly at the stars above, but he still felt Oliver flinch at his words. "I've seen so many fools lose their livelihoods—even a couple lose their very lives—over something as frivolous as love. I never understood it. I'm sure you've seen similar things."

Oliver said nothing, but Tameer saw him nod out of the corner of his eye. "It's baffling, really. How people can let something so silly wreck their entire world."

Clearing his throat, Oliver opened his mouth to say something, but Tameer wasn't finished. "I think the most outrageous thing about it all is that no matter how hard one tries to avoid it, love still manages to get its claws into people. Upending their lives in the most unexpected ways." Tameer kicked his feet in the cool water, splashing as he pondered his next words. He'd been debating how—or even *if*—he should say anything, but decided saying nothing would be the coward's way out. Tameer had never been a coward before. No reason to start now.

Pulling one leg up, he turned to face Oliver, giving the man his full attention. "I love you. Isn't that the worst thing you've ever heard? I would happily let you ruin my life without a second thought. Hells, I'd burn this entire warehouse to the ground and follow you and your family wherever you choose to go, if I thought that's what you wanted."

Tameer watched Oliver's face, looking for even the slightest hint that Oliver might feel the same way. Either the man had the best poker face in the world, or Tameer had read the situation entirely wrong. Oliver's face was utterly blank. His mouth hung slightly open as he stared at Tameer.

Fuck. He'd known this was a possibility, but it still fucking hurt. Like having his heart ripped from his chest, frozen in ice, shattered to pieces, and then having those shards shoved back into his chest. Fuck fuck fuck.

Nodding once, he tried to school his face once more, mimicking Oliver's blank stare. "Right then. I guess I'll see you around." Turning away, Tameer tried to ignore the ache in his chest. He'd been rejected before and survived. He'd survive this, too. He'd be fine. Eventually. He always was.

A hand wrapped around Tameer's wrist. "Where the hells do you think you're going?" Oliver's voice was rough. Raw with emotion. Tameer turned back to see tears glistening in the man's eyes. "You just drop a bomb like that and expect to up and walk away? No, sir. I don't think so." Oliver tugged Tameer's arm, pulling him back down.

Tameer reached out with his free hand, skillfully sliding his fingers into Oliver's hair and tugging, tilting the man's head back. "Is there something you wanted to say?" he challenged.

Oliver grunted, stretching his legs out and pulling Tameer down onto his lap. His fingers dug into Tameer's ass, claiming him with his touch while reaching up with his lips, desperate to own his mouth as well.

"Use your words, darling," Tameer teased, keeping his lips just out of reach. "I can't understand grunts."

Oliver growled, squeezing Tameer's ass tighter, but conceded. "I love you, you troublesome man. Now let me kiss you before I flip you over and punish you instead."

Tameer chuckled, leaning in for the briefest of kisses before moving his lips to Oliver's ear. "Don't threaten me with a good time," he whispered, giving a teasing nibble to his earlobe.

18

Oliver toyed with Tameer's hair as he contemplated their next move. Mom and Pop were recovering, and they'd already expressed a desire to stay at the Guild's headquarters for a while. Mom had nearly collapsed at the sight of Matty, healthy and completely cured. She'd held him for so long, Pop had to pry him from her just to get to her to eat something. Once she'd learned Leah was the one to provide the cure, she'd wrapped the assassin in an equally thorough embrace. It was sweet, honestly, but Oliver would never vocalize that.

"Roach and Hellbore are sly. They'll be able to suss out my would-be usurpers by the end of the day." Tameer sounded far more confident than Oliver felt. He didn't trust anyone in that godsforsaken place.

"How can you be so sure they aren't a part of the plot?"

Tameer chuckled, shifting his head on Oliver's shoulder as he curled tighter against him in their bed. "You mean besides the fact that Roach literally offered her life to me and I *didn't* kill her?"

Oliver huffed. "That's still fucking weird, by the way."

Tameer continued as though he hadn't heard Oliver's comment. "Roach and Hellbore were two of the first kids that benefitted from my restrictions about child labor. They were raised here, but never forced into Guild business until after I was kicked out. They're old enough to remember what it was like when I was still here and in charge. They were safe under my protection. They suffered when I left. They're loyal, trust me."

Oliver grunted but didn't reply. He didn't trust anyone until they'd earned it. He'd been burned too many times in the past. "What about your third name? The third person on your list of supposedly trustworthy people in this damn place?"

Tameer turned his head, quicker than Oliver imagined the man could move, and bit Oliver's shoulder hard enough to elicit an unexpected groan. Pulling back, an impish spark light Tameer's eyes. "This damn place is my home now. Yours too, I hope. You should be nicer."

Oliver instantly grabbed a fistful of Tameer's hair, forcing his lips back to the shoulder now baring teeth marks. Whispering harshly in Tameer's ear, Oliver commanded, "I'll say what I please. You might be the king of this *damn* place, but I bow to no one." Nipping Tameer's ear to emphasize his words, Oliver smirked at the answering groan that escaped Tam's soft lips.

Releasing his hold on the man, Oliver lounged back on the bed once more, giving Tameer the same cocky grin Tam had just tried to give him. "You were say?" he prompted. "About the third person."

Tameer blinked, rolling his neck and clearly trying to refocus his mind. Oh, yes, Oliver was definitely winning whatever game they were playing today. He loved it.

"Right. Alec. We came up together in the Guild. He hated the old ways as much as I did." Tameer ran a hand through his hair, brushing it back from his eyes and sitting up in their bed. "He should be back with news soon. I spoke with him last night, when we got back. He's a thief, although not a terribly good one. Too cocky and not nearly cautious enough. But he's an excellent spy. That man can creep through halls like a damn ghost."

"Sounds like that would make him an excellent thief." Oliver pulled himself into a seated position as well. Their bed was more of a pallet stuffed with hay on the floor, but it was in one of the few rooms with four walls on the second floor of the warehouse, so it was private.

Tameer chuckled ruefully, reaching over to pull a bit of hay from Oliver's hair. "It should. The problem is, once Alec gets in and gets his prize, he gets cocky. He isn't careful on his exit. He's been caught more times than anyone else in the Guild. Combined."

Well, that would be problematic, Oliver thought. A thief who often got caught wasn't a thief worth keeping around, but he didn't bother voicing that opinion. Clearly, Tameer was emotionally attached to this Alec, or he would've cut ties with the man long ago. And if he turned out to have useful intel, who was Oliver to argue?

Tameer sat anxiously behind the slightly rotten wooden table serving as his desk, mindlessly staring out the broken window, awaiting news. Oliver had invited him to lunch with his family, but Tameer was in no mood for friendly family conversations, not to mention, Oliver deserved some quality time with his parents. They had a lot to catch up on. Tameer didn't want to get in the way.

Still, it was nice to be invited. He appreciated the offer and made sure Oliver knew it.

Now, though, Tameer's mind was a jumble of dark thoughts and deeper fears. Waiting for news from Roach, Hellbore, and Alec was torture. He almost wished he had gone with Oliver, just to have a distraction from the weight of a coup hanging over his head.

Voices echoed down the hall, drawing Tameer's attention. Sitting upright, he tried to look more confident than he currently felt. Gods, he'd thought coming back to the Guild would be smooth, easy even. He'd been so fucking arrogant.

"So I said, 'What are you gonna do? Shoot me?' and the bastard actually took a shot!" Alec raised his tunic, showing off a still-healing wound. From across the room, Tameer couldn't see the wound well, but he speculated it was the result of a crossbow bolt rather than an arrow.

Hellbore cackled, slapping Alec on the back and shaking his head. "It's a miracle yer still alive. Dumbass."

"Madame Luck has a thing for me," Alec replied with an exaggerated wink to Roach.

Roach—much to Tameer's surprise—flushed a vibrant pink, quickly looking away and crossing the room to join Tameer at his desk. "Got news, boss," she said briskly, nodding to a chair as though asking permission to sit.

Tameer gestured for her to take a seat while Alec and Hellbore made themselves at home on the moth-eaten couch near the cold hearth. "What have you heard?"

"Nyx wants you gone." Roach was never one to mince words. It was one of the things Tam had always liked about her. "She was Sigrun's right hand and had been planning to take over from him. Seems she's keeping those plans and has you in her sights now."

"Literally?" Tameer asked. It was a valid question, after all. He needed to know if Nyx was any good with distance kills. It would effect how he'd adjust until things were handled.

"Nah," Hellbore answered, throwing an arm over the back of the couch. "She's more of an up-close and personal type. She stab you in the back while smiling at your face."

Alec huffed. "What the hells does that mean? Is she a contortionist? How can she stab someone in the back *while* facing them?"

Hellbore stared dumbfounded for a second, then slapped Alec on the back of the head. "It's just a saying, smartass. I wasn't being literal. Fuck."

The two continued to bicker, but Tameer tuned them out. Nyx. He didn't remember her, which meant she was new to the Guild. Well, "new" as in new in the last few years, but she'd clearly risen through the ranks quickly if she'd been Sigrun's right hand. But not a trustworthy right hand, as she'd already been plotting to take him out.

Tameer interrupted the incessant chatter with more pertinent questions. "Where does she hunt? Does she sleep here? What's her primary game?"

Alec stood, dusting his trousers off and giving a disgusted look at the couch. "Nyx doesn't sleep here. She's got her own place, but no one knows where. She prefers to do most of her work in the royal and high-end merchant district of Ravendale, but for the right price, she'll go anywhere. Typically, she's a jewel thief, but again, for the right price, she'll steal anything. I even heard a few stories of her nicking paintings, and one of her kidnapping a dog."

"A dog?" Roach's confusion was written all over her face. "What the hells for?"

Alec shrugged. "Coin? Someone paid her, I'd imagine."

"How do ye wanna handle this, boss?" Hellbore asked, now fully stretched out on the couch, head laying on the armrest, feet crossed on the other.

Alec opened his mouth to offer a solution, but Tameer already had a plan forming in his mind.

"She goes after shiny things, so let's give her something shiny, yeah?"

Tameer sent a raven to Irena. Coded, naturally. Nyx would be headed her way. He had let it slip that the Queen had a very sparkly, *very* gaudy crown she never wore, collecting dust in a closet in the little Prince's room. As easy as it would have been to let Leah handle Nyx—as Alec had been eager to suggest—Tameer didn't want to depend on Leah's violence to maintain his authority in the Guild.

While he didn't want to rule by fear, Tameer understood that there needed to be clear consequences for actions made against him. Plotting his murder was definitely something he couldn't take likely. Setting up his would-be murderer for decades in prison seemed like a fair punishment.

Oliver had argued that Tameer should have killed the woman himself, but after the blood rage that had coursed through him while fighting and slaughtering Sigrun, Tameer wasn't sure he'd ever be ready to take a life again.

19

I T TOOK A FEW days for Roach and Hellbore to collect all the supplies that Mom needed to start smithing, but Oliver didn't mind. He and Tameer had plenty of ways to entertain themselves.

Construction had begun on the interior of the warehouse, rebuilding the walls to make the building structurally sound again. It was messy and loud, but so were Tameer and Oliver, so he wasn't one to complain. Leah and Ash headed back to Vexia after Mom and Pop got settled. Tam had been pretty disappointed that they hadn't stayed longer, but Leah promised to visit soon. It was only a day-trip by boat, after all. She even offered to bring cinnamon rolls on their next trip.

Within a week of freeing Mom and Pop, the merchant who'd been holding them hostage had filed a formal complaint. Before Oliver's anxiety could even begin to get the better of him, Tameer had spoken with Queen Irena and gotten the charges dismissed. He'd argued that Oliver's parents were acting under duress and never would have attempted to rob the merchant if not for the former Guild leader's coercion. The rug merchant had been livid, but there was nothing he could do. A pardon from the Queen Mother was undeniable. His parents were free to resume their life of crime as they saw fit.

At the moment, though, they were living crime-free lives as smiths and metal workers for the Guild. Well, Mom was. Pop was training the newest guild members in the art of the grift. They were both still far thinner and paler than Oliver would have liked, but they were recovering quickly, thanks to the Guild. Matty had even started working with the twins on a regular basis.

Oliver wasn't sure he loved the idea, but Matty was learning new skills, honing his own craft, and having a great time. Plus, it kept him from hitting on unavailable women and getting his ass beat.

Thunder crashed in the distance as Oliver gazed out the window of the room he now shared with Tameer.

"Probably should have gotten the roof fixed first," Tameer grumbled, coming up to stand beside Oliver, glaring out at the heavy clouds looming in the distance.

"The contractor said there was no point putting a new hat on a rotting whore." He was quite the colorful character, their contractor. Oliver draped an arm across Tameer's shoulders, pressing a kiss to his temple. "We'll be fine. The first floor stays dry enough. We can all sleep down there tonight if it gets too bad."

Tameer sighed, nodding glumly. He enjoyed their private space. Hells, so did Oliver, but he also enjoyed sleeping in a dry bed, not a lake.

"Mom said she should get to the rings today." Oliver changed the subject to one he knew would cheer Tameer up. It turned out, Mom was actually a very skilled smith, once she got back in the practice. She'd made the earrings Tam had requested without any problem and had readily accepted a second job to make some emerald rings.

"Wonderful! I know just the merchant's wife to sell them to." A sly, foxlike grin split his face.

They hadn't talked about the future. Tameer was too afraid to fuck anything up by broaching the subject. Oliver seemed very happy with the Guild. Hells, his whole family was thriving there, as far as Tam could tell, but he didn't want to pressure them to stay. Tam had meant it when he'd said he would leave with Oliver if that's what he wanted.

Tameer understood now why fools rushed in. Why love made people do things that, outwardly, looked insane or idiotic. He would do anything to see Oliver smile. To wake up beside that man every day for the rest of his life. If Oliver chose to return to his nomadic life with his family, Tameer would willingly go with him. Assuming he was invited, of course.

"What do you think, boss?" Chantrelle offered him two of the finest gold rings he'd ever seen. The tear-drop emeralds were perfectly placed and sparkled like magic.

"They're stunning, Chantrelle. And I've told you, you don't have to call me that. Please, just Tam."

Chantrelle clucked her tongue, turning back to her forge and stirring the coals. Adding a few more fragments of silver to the pot of molten metal, she turned back to face Tameer, hand on hip as she studied him.

Tameer instantly felt nervous. This woman had an eye like no other. She could spot a mark from a hundred yards away. She'd find any flaw in him and call him out on it in a heartbeat. Oliver was casually perusing the gemstones lined up along the windowsill, clearly unaware of his mother's predatory inspection.

"I've been thinking about what comes next," she began slowly.

Oliver immediately perked up. He set the sapphire he'd been admiring back down and joined Tameer and his mother. "Got plans already?"

"Your father and I were talking last night," she continued, turning her back to stir the molten metal, adding a few more slivers of silver. "What if we stayed here?"

Her back was to them as she spoke, but Tameer got the feeling she was nervous about something. Either his response or Oliver's reaction. Maybe both.

Oliver reacted first.

"What the hells are you talking about, Mom? You never stay in one place for more than a month."

Chantrelle faced her son, and a single eyebrow raised.

Oliver's cheeks brightened ever-so-slightly. "Sorry, I just mean, you and Pop are mobile people. We've always moved around a lot. What changed?"

She shrugged casually. "I'm feeling rooty."

A laugh escaped Tameer's lips before he could stop it. He quickly covered his mouth, trying to recapture the sound, but it was too late. "Sorry," he muttered.

Chantrelle gave him a warm smile. "It's fine, boss," she said with a wink. "It just feels like time to stop and be still. At least for a while. Enoki is having so much fun teaching the next generation. Matty is doing well with the twins. I've forgotten how much I love smithing. Not to mention you two." Tears welled in her eyes as she looked on at them. "When we were in that cell"—her voice cracked, emotion clogging her throat for a moment. Swallowing hard, she shook her head and continued. "When we were locked up, I was worried we'd never see you boys again. Worried you'd spent your whole lives running and never have a chance to find what me and your dad have. But I see it now, with the two of you. Oli, I'm so happy for you." Silent tears slide down her face, answered by tears on Tam's. "I'm not ready to leave yet. Maybe one day, but if it's all right with you both, we'd like to stick around for a while."

Tameer was at a loss for words. Instead, he wrapped the woman in his arms, hugging her and welcoming her into his own little family of misfits and thieves.

"So you're staying, huh?" Tameer brushed a hand through Oliver's dark hair. They laid on the straw-filled mattress in their room. Oliver's head rested on Tameer's chest, listening to the steady *thump thump thump* of his heart.

Eyes half closed as he basked in the soothing feeling on Tam's fingers in his hair and his warm body beneath him, it took a second for Oliver to realize he was meant to respond.

Shifting, he put his hand on Tam's chest, resting his chin on the back of it and looked into Tameer's eyes. "Are you okay with that?"

Warmth filled Tam's gaze before he even opened his mouth. Oh, yeah, he was good with it. "Of course," he said softly, his eyes flicking from Oliver's to his lips and back again. "I go where you go, right?"

Grinning, Oliver pushed up, pressing a possessive kiss to Tameer's lips, commanding entry and leaving him breathless. Pulling back after a moment, Oliver smiled down at the disheveled look on his lover's face. "That's my line."

NOT reaDY TO LeaVe VeXIa YeT?

Want to see where it all began? Go back to the beginning with Leah's story!

Enemies to lovers

Retired assassin turned small-town baker

vs

Captain of the King's Guard

Snarky

Steamy

And delicious cinnamon rolls

<u>Of Poison and Passion</u>

Or dive into Irena's story!

Fake engagement.
Royal intrigue.
He falls first (**hard**).
Celtic and Greek influence.
And romance. Steam, but no spice.

<u>The Royal Gambit</u>

Also by Mallory Wanless

The *turmio* trilogy:
Storm and Flame: Enchanted I
Blood and Destiny: Enchanted II
Reign and Ruin: Enchanted III

Enchanted Standalones:
Reclaiming the Frost: Enchanted IV

Vexia Standalone Novellas:
Of Poison and Passion
The Royal Gambit
The Marked and The Menaced

Mallory lives in Texas with her husband and their two young boys. She spends her days home-schooling and full-time parenting. Her nights, and any free time she manages to carve out during the day, are devoted to reading and writing.

If you enjoy this story, please be sure to leave a review on your favorite sites. Thank you so much!